Dragon's Stone

JENA WADE

Table of Contents

[Title Page](#)

[Copyright](#)

[Chapter One](#)

[Chapter Two](#)

[Chapter Three](#)

[Chapter Four](#)

[Chapter Five](#)

[Chapter Six](#)

[Chapter Seven](#)

[Chapter Eight](#)

[Chapter Nine](#)

[More From Jena Wade](#)

[About Jena Wade](#)

Dragon's Stone

Dragons

Book Three

Jena Wade

Copyright © 2019 by Jena Wade

All rights reserved. This copy is intended for the original purchaser of this book ONLY. No part of this book may be reproduced, scanned, or distributed in any printed or electronic form without prior written permission from the author. Please do not participate in or encourage piracy of copyrighted materials in violation of the author's rights. Purchase only authorized editions.

Image/art disclaimer: Licensed material is being used for illustrative purposes only. Any person depicted in the licensed material is a model.

Published in the United States of America

This book is a work of fiction. While reference might be made to actual historical events or existing locations, the names, characters, places and incidents are either the product of the author's imagination or are used fictitiously, and any resemblance to actual persons, living or dead, business establishments, events, or locales is entirely coincidental.

www.thejenawade.com

Warning

This book contains sexually explicit scenes and adult language and may be considered offensive to some readers. Jena Wade's books are for sale to adults ONLY, as defined by the laws of the country in which you made your purchase. Please store your files wisely, where they cannot be accessed by under-aged readers.

Chapter One

Mason

I sat at the edge of the pond on the wolf pack property, skipping stones, pocketing ones I could use later for carving. I tried to keep my mind blank—not thinking about him. My mate. The one that rejected me.

For the past ten years, while living with the wolf pack, I'd dreamt of finding a mate, belonging to another person, being their one and only. I'd fantasized about it for years. I'd even saved my virginity for the possibility of having a mate someday, only to find out my mate was not a wolf like I'd assumed he'd be. My mate was a dragon; and a mean one at that.

The only memory I had of Broderick was him glaring at me, then storming out of the room. That was the only time I'd seen him. I wish now that I'd never met him, never known this pull I felt toward him. Toward a man who didn't even want me.

It had been two months since I'd left Dragon Headquarters, as the five remaining dragons in the world affectionately referred to their compound. The place reminded me a lot of our wolf pack's compound. It had been quite an adjustment at age fourteen to learn that wolf-shifters and other paranormal type creatures existed in the world.

I'd never forget the night that my adopted mother explained it all to me. She sat me down, told me about wolf-shifters and witches, and then asked if I was sure I wanted to be adopted by them. Of course I wanted to be adopted. I wanted a family more than anything in the world. I couldn't care less if they turned into wolves or chickens or ducks. They were family.

I didn't know who my biological parents were. The records were sealed, and I saw no reason to go out looking for them. After all, they had abandoned me at birth. Why would they want me now that I was grown?

"Hey," a voice said.

I recognized it immediately as my adopted brother Jericho, the Alpha of our pack.

"Hey," I said. I continued to stare at the pond, not taking my eyes off the flat water.

Jericho sat down next to me. "I'm taking you back to Dragon Headquarters."

I whipped my head around. "What? Why?"

Jericho took a deep breath and sat up straight, it was a motion that I'd seen him do plenty of times, when he was centering himself to defend a decision he'd made as our Alpha. A decision that not everyone would agree with. "Technically, you are one of the dragons' mates. And I think you should spend some time with Broderick, to see if you two can work things out."

"No." I shook my head. "He doesn't want me. He doesn't want a mate at all. I'm not going to force it. And I don't want to be around him." *Don't want to be rejected by him again.*

"I understand that, but there's also the fact that you're a dragon's mate and Molpe is out there kidnapping dragons' mates. You'll be safer there. Molpe already admitted that she and her vampire can't break into their property. Whereas here, they've already kidnapped from our compound once. I don't want to take that risk."

"Then why let me stay here for the past two months if you were just going to send me back there?"

Jericho ran a hand through his hair. "I'd hoped that your mate would come to his senses, but he hasn't yet. He hasn't even returned to their property."

My shoulders sagged. I wasn't going to change his mind. "I still don't understand why I have to go."

"It's just temporary," Jericho said. "I want you to be safe, and we're wearing ourselves pretty thin having extra guards posted for every shift."

That was news to me. "You've had the betas running extra shifts?"

Jericho nodded. "I don't want to take any chances with your safety. With Molpe still at large, we need to remain vigilant."

My stomached tightened into knots. While I'd sat around the last two months moping about my mate not wanting me, the rest of the pack had pulled double-duty to keep me safe. I felt like a tool.

"I'll bring you back home once we take care of Molpe and that vampire, I promise."

"I'll go. When do we leave?" I asked. I couldn't let my pack suffer for my safety.

"In a of couple hours. I've got to check on Cody and make sure his care is set up."

I nodded. Cody still hadn't come out of his coma. But thanks to the fluids and rest he was getting, his vitals remained stable and he'd put on some weight. He'd been kidnapped over a year ago by Molpe. It was only when Gale, one of the dragons, had been tricked into going to Molpe's cave that he was rescued.

"I have to run to the shop," I said. "Pick up my tools. I don't know how long I'll be gone, so I'll make arrangements with Patty."

Jericho stood. "All right, I'll meet you at the house in a bit then, okay?" He laid a hand on my shoulder and I looked up at him. "It's going to be okay, Mason. I promise. I know it seems bleak now, having a mate that you can't reach out to, but it's going to get better. It has to get better."

I forced a smile. "Thanks, Jericho."

He nodded and turned away.

I felt like an ass. I wasn't the only one in the world with a mate they couldn't actually connect with.

I'd long suspected that Cody was Jericho's mate, and seeing the anguish he'd gone through the past several months only confirmed it for me.

I stood up, dusted myself off, and squared my shoulders. If I was going to face my mate, I would do it with my head held high. Although, I had no idea what I would say to him if he was standing in front of me right now. Maybe I'd ask him why. Was it me or him?

I'm going to assume it's him.

I made my way back to the compound and grabbed the keys to my car. It was a Chevy Aveo, a compact car, but quite functional and it got great gas mileage, which worked out well living forty-five minutes from everywhere.

When I arrived at the store where I sold some of my carvings, Patty was working the front desk. She waved hello to me and I waved back. I made a beeline for the backroom, so I could grab my tools and be on my way. Of course, I'd let Patty know that I'd be leaving, but I wanted to be as quick as I could.

When I went back into the front room, she had just finished with her customer.

"Hi, Patty," I said.

"Hi, Mason." She didn't smile, her eyes had a misty look to them, like she held back tears.

"What is it?" I asked.

"Jericho called me and told me that you'd be gone for a little while."

"Yeah," I said. "Apparently I'm going to go stay with the dragons. It'll give me a chance to hang out with my brother, Frost. That will be nice."

She smiled. "Yeah, but we'll miss you around here."

"I'll be back, eventually," I said. I had no expectations that Broderick would see me for the second time and determine that I was worthy of being his mate, or get over whatever the fuck his hang-up was. If he didn't want me, I wasn't going to dwell on it. I'd continue living my life.

"You'll still send me some of your work, right?" She asked.

"Yeah, some of the smaller pieces should ship easily enough, and we can always post the bigger ones online and I can ship them to the buyer from wherever the heck I'm gonna be."

"Okay," she said. "Give me a hug before you go."

She hugged me tightly and gave me a kiss on the cheek. "Be a good boy."

"Okay." I smiled. I had long since stopped being a boy, but that's okay. "I promise."

As I left the shop, I ran right into another person I needed to say goodbye to. Instantly I recognized the thick cologne.

"Peter," I said. "I'm glad I ran into you."

Peter had been one of my regular customers for the past two months. He always came in to see what my latest piece was. For a brief moment, I'd thought maybe he had some sort of romantic interest in me. But he'd never crossed the line from friendly to anything else. So, I must have been mistaken. Not that I was interested anyway. Having a mate out there meant that I wasn't going to be with anyone else, ever. Whether my mate claimed me or not, I'd be loyal to him.

"Oh?" Peter raised a dark brow. His black hair was short and always perfectly cut and styled. It matched his pale face and high cheekbones. The man could be a model for something luxurious, Gucci or Calvin Klein. He had always struck me as sophisticated, though I didn't know what he did as a career. "Where are you headed off to? Shouldn't you be working right now?"

"No," I shook my head. "I'm going out of town for a little bit. I don't know when I'll be back."

"Oh, really?" He asked. The corner of his lips twitched like he was going to smile, but he didn't. "Still pining for that guy you told me about? Please don't tell me you're going to let him get away with how he treated you?"

Something told me to keep my exact destination a secret, after all, this man wasn't a pack member. He was just friendly. I'd told him a humanized version of my interaction with Broderick, without explaining that we were mates and destined to be together.

I shrugged. "Just hanging out with some friends out east."

That was the general direction I'd be going, but it was about as a vague as I could be.

The wind picked up at that moment and blew his coat open. He wore a pair of dark slacks, with a black t-shirt. My eyes were immediately drawn to his necklace. A deep purple crystal hung from a chain around his neck. When he caught me staring, he closed his coat.

"I'll miss you." He stepped toward me and I almost took a step back instinctually, like he was some sort of predator, but I stopped myself.

I smiled. It felt nice to be wanted, knowing that someone wanted to be around me even my mate didn't.

"Well, Patty will still have all of my work here for you to take a look at, and as a regular you can have first dibs, I promise."

"Oh, I won't just be missing your work, Mason. I'll be missing you as well."

My cheeks burned with a blush that made me want to cringe. I didn't know what to say to that, so I just smiled. "Well, I've got to get going. Jericho is waiting for me."

"Here," he said. "Take my card." He pulled out a business card and scribbled a number on the back. "That's my personal cell. Text me or call me sometime. At least let me know when you'll be back in town."

"All right," I said. "I'll do that." I pulled out my phone and entered his number, then sent him a quick, "Hi."

"There. Now you've got my number too."

"Excellent." He grinned wide, his pearly white teeth practically shining in the sunlight. Much to my surprise, he gave me a quick hug and kissed my cheek. "I'll really miss you, Mason."

"I'll miss you, too," I said and walked away.

***

Jericho was waiting outside our house with a suitcase next to him when I got back to the compound.

"Are we taking my car?" I asked.

He nodded, picked up the suitcase, and tossed it in the trunk. "Yeah. I figured you would need a car there."

"How are you going to get back?"

"Armant is coming back with me. We'll be flying."

My eyes widened. "You get to fly on a dragon? Do you think—" I bit my lip and looked down.

"You want to fly on a dragon?" He grinned.

"Yeah," I said. "It would be amazing. Do you think one of them will let me?"

His smile fell. "I'm not sure that's the best idea. Unless—"

"Unless Broderick says it's okay." I wanted to roll my eyes, but I knew it would be disrespectful to him as both my brother and Alpha of the pack.

"Yeah, I doubt he'll let you fly on any other dragon."

"Well, then I just won't ask his permission. I am sure one of the others will let me."

I went inside and quickly packed up some clothes and any personal items I would need. I made sure to have my spare set of tools and my sketchbook. I would have a lot of time on my hands at Dragon Headquarters. I could get quite a bit of work done. Maybe they would let me explore the property and see what sort of stone I could find to carve.

Jericho leaned against the driver's side door when I walked out again, suitcase in hand. He grabbed the suitcase from me, then paused.

"What?" I asked.

He shook he head. "Nothing. Just thought I smelled something, but it's gone now. You don't have to go, you know," he said. "I'm not forcing you. You just say the word and you can stay here, we'll make something work."

I nodded. "I know. But it's not fair to the pack for me to cause so much extra work. If it's too hard to be there, to be around Broderick, I'll come home. I promise."

"I really think Broderick just needs time. There is no way to deny the mate pull, at least not for wolf shifters. I doubt dragons are any different. The Fates didn't give us these gifts for us to deny them."

I shrugged one shoulder, unsure of what to say. Not being a shifter myself, it was hard to understand. While I did feel the pull toward Broderick, it was manageable, and largely overshadowed by the fact that he had stormed out of the room at the first sight of me. It was hard to imagine coming back from that.

I hopped into the passenger side. Jericho slid into the driver's seat.

"I'll take the first shift," he said. "You can navigate."

"Onward to adventure," I said and smiled, though my heart wasn't in it.

Chapter Two

Broderick

I slung the jackhammer over my shoulder and walked it back to where we kept the tools. The day was hot, but the job was done, the only thing that stood between me and a cold beer was a hell of a long drive.

"Hey, Brody. You off on vacation now?"

"Yep," I said and wiped the sweat off my forehead. I slipped off the orange safety vest that was necessary for my construction job and tossed it in the back of the truck. "Taking some time off for some R and R," I said. I wasn't sure if I would be back to this particular job. It was hard to tell these days just how much time I would spend at Dragon Headquarters. Since that bitch Molpe decided to wreak havoc on our lives, we made sure to have at least three of us there at all times.

"Gonna get some fishing in?"

"Hell yeah," I said. I didn't know if I would actually do any fishing in human form, but my dragon loved to fish.

"Take it easy, man."

"Thanks," I said. I hopped in the truck. I'd been avoiding headquarters for the past two months because when I was there, I spent way too much time thinking about him. My mate. Mason.

I'd only seen him the one time, but his face would forever be etched in my brain. He was the timid sort, careful how he walked in the room. Eyeing everyone and taking stock of who was around. His dark brown eyes matched well with his dark brown hair that he kept slightly long. It curled around his collar. He had a slimmer build than me, though I suppose everybody did. I had the build of an individual who spent four hours a day lifting weights. I barely did anything to maintain my muscle mass, it simply came naturally being a stone dragon. The brutes of the dragon species.

Our size had served us well when dragons had been plentiful, but it had been used as a weapon during the war. I didn't like to think about that time. It was a toss-up between what was more painful to think about: the war two thousand years ago or having a mate in present day.

I stepped into my truck and began the long trek back to headquarters. I suppose I could put the truck in the garage at my house and fly, but I might as well have my truck with me. Besides, being in my dragon form meant that I'd be that much closer to my natural instincts, which meant I'd have a harder time denying the attraction I felt toward Mason.

I let out a sigh, knowing that I wasn't going to be able to block the vision of him in my mind for much longer. Sooner or later I was going to cave and go to him.

I clenched my jaw.

No. I could fight this pull.

I'd seen Leonidas and Gale find their mates and witnessed the aftermath of dealing with Flint being kidnapped, and Gale being captured by Molpe. All of it resulting in unnecessary heartache. I didn't need to be reminded what loss felt like. I relived it in my dreams every night. Two thousand years had not diluted the pain at all. Having a mate meant opening myself up to heartache and pain. I'd seen it firsthand with my brother and with my friends, and I didn't want it. I was perfectly content living a regular middle-class life, working construction jobs around the country, operating heavy machinery, destroying things and building them back up again. I'd long since learned to ignore my desire to build a family.

A family with Mason. The vision came out of nowhere. Brown hair, curly, dark brown eyes, long eye lashes, chubby baby cheeks. Mason would make a cute baby, that's for sure. I couldn't help but smile. I wanted to kick myself. I wasn't supposed to be thinking about that. I needed to think about the fact that Mason was human. Weak. Breakable. Fragile.

If Molpe got her hands on him, he'd be toast in an instant. If that vampire got near him… It would just take one bite and Mason would be gone, drained of blood and life. Taken from me before I could even do anything about it.

So why the hell did you leave him unprotected for the past two months?

I blew out a breath. It had been hard for me to come to terms with the fact that my mate was being protected by someone other than myself. He was my mate. My responsibility. But then again, if we were the only ones who knew that Mason was a dragon's mate, then Molpe would have no reason to go after him.

If I stayed away, he would be safe. Molpe had no idea that he was my mate. How could she?

Plus, he lived with a wolf pack. They would keep him safe.

I'd heard from Gale and Frost that Jericho had increased the security around their compound. Merek had even given them additional surveillance supplies; cameras, motion detectors. Mason was safe with them. I knew he and Frost talked every day.

Once I got to the house, I put my tools away in the garage. I wouldn't be needing them for a while since I would be here for at least a month. I tossed my duffel bag in my room, not bothering to put anything away. I didn't have many clothes or things to keep around. At my age, you'd think I would have collected a few more belongings, but I was a simple dragon. I liked my simple life and thank God for the invention of jeans and white t-shirts that came in packs of five.

I went down to the kitchen and found Armant there, staring into the fridge.

"Any good food?" I asked.

"No," he said. "Leonidas and Flint went out to get groceries. Frost has both kids in the library."

"Seems like a legit place for them to hang out."

"We call it a library, but it seems to have been overtaken by baby things," Armant said with a bit of distaste in his voice.

"Maybe we should set up a playroom for the kids. We could take out the east wall and have the sitting room be a little play area for all the dragon babies that are running around this place."

"All two of them?" Armant raised an eyebrow. "Or are we making plans for when your dragon baby comes in the picture?"

"Don't start with me," I said.

Merek came in the room. "Oh, good, you're here. Broderick, I need to talk to you about Mason."

"Not you, too," I said. "Can you guys just give me a break? I don't want to talk about Mason." Just saying his name out loud sent a shiver down my spine. His name sounded sexy on my lips. I kind of wondered what my name would sound like on his. Late at night. Moaned in pleasure.

I rolled my eyes. Goddess bless. I was going soft. I'd spent too much time around the mated dragons.

Gale came in. "Broderick, I thought I heard your voice. I was just about to—"

"Stop right there." I held up my hand and faced all three of them, my closest friends. "If you're going to say something about Mason, I don't want to hear it. How many times do I have to tell you all, I do not want a mate. Especially not some human who grew up with a wolf pack. Mason is scrawny, weak, and breakable. The dude would break under me. I might as well put a 'fragile' stamp on his forehead. I don't know what the hell the Fates were thinking when they decided that he was *right* for me. They must have made a mistake. He can't possibly be my mate. I don't want a mate. I have no need for one. And if I was going to pick out a mate, he would be way different than Mason. Mason is…." I stopped cold when my eyes locked on the narrow gaze of the only man in the world who could get my pulse racing—Mason.

"Walking into the room right now," Merek said.

Oh, fuck. My stomach dropped like a stone. Oh fuck. I'd gone too far. Never mind the fact that I didn't mean anything that I'd said. The look on Mason's face told me that he'd heard it. The tan glow that he usually had faded away. He'd gone completely pale, and his eyes narrowed to thin slits.

He walked over to me and lifted his chin. I didn't even see the hand come up until I felt the sting on my face from the slap.

"You're no prize either," he bit out, then ran from the room.

I touched a hand to my cheek, feeling a welt there already. It burned, but I deserved every bit of it. I met the eyes of Merek, Armant, and Gale all of them staring at me, wide eyed.

"All right then," I said, and I left the room.

Chapter Three

Mason

I ran, heading straight for the woods behind the property.

As soon as I heard the things Broderick had to say about me, about having a mate, I wanted to escape. Growing up in a wolf pack with hormonal shifters full of angst, I'd learned how to get in touch with nature. Young shifters were encouraged to run off their energy by escaping into the woods around the pack compound. They meditated in the woods so they could think and clear their minds.

I'd adopted the same habit.

I didn't want to hear any more about how Broderick felt about having a mate. So, I ran, and I just kept running, leaping over tree limbs, branches slapping me in the face, leaving scratches along my arms and cheeks. I didn't care, I just wanted to get away.

I came across an open meadow filled with wild flowers, and I stopped running. In the meadow was an odd arrangement of boulders and slabs of large flat rocks almost arranged in a pattern to make a square surface. It was an odd setup and seemed a bit out of place. The rocks were warm to the touch, but it looked like as good a place as any to sit and think before I returned to the house, or I could just make my home permanently out here.

I climbed up and sat cross legged on the top foundation. I closed my eyes, inhaled through my nose, and exhaled through my mouth. Meditation was a form of control taught to young shifters in order to get in touch with their inner wolf. I didn't have an inner wolf, but the practice still helped. I tried to clear my mind of everything, but one thought played on a loop. *Weak. Fragile. Breakable. Human.* As if I hadn't grown up with the knowledge that I was *just* human. My family amongst the wolf pack had never made me feel that being human made me anything less than what they were. I was just different, and different was perfectly okay. With Broderick, it sounded like different was wrong.

A shadow fell over me and I looked up to the sky to see a ginormous mass circling above. My heart kicked up a notch, not in fear, but in excitement. That was my dragon up there, circling. My body betrayed me once again. I wanted to know what he looked like in dragon form. I wanted to see *my* dragon.

The ground shook, and a puff of air hit me as Broderick touched down. His dragon was gorgeous, about the size of a two-story farmhouse. He had brown scales and a long, thick tail for balancing I assumed. That's what I had heard the dinosaurs used their tails for, so it would make sense that dragons were the same way.

"I just want to be left alone. Fuck off," I said.

Quick as a blink, Broderick transformed back into his human form. He was naked, I should have looked away, but I didn't want to appear even weaker, so I forced myself to stare at him. At his face, not anything else, though. I wanted to drop my gaze lower, but I didn't. He didn't need to know that I wanted him, despite what he had said about me.

"Please," I said. "You've made your feelings quite clear, and I think it would be best if we just didn't spend any time around one another." I turned then and faced the other direction, hoping that he would respect my wishes and leave. I should have known better.

Broderick climbed on to the boulder and sat next to me. He'd dressed himself in a pair of pants that he'd somehow managed to bring with him.

I closed my eyes and sighed. "I've never been violent toward another person before in my life," I said. "Never once hit another person out of anger. I didn't even know I had it in me. I'm sorry that you happened to be in the way of me expressing my feelings."

"Don't apologize," Broderick said. His deep voice was soft, almost timid, and I looked over at him. His face still had quite a welt on it. It surprised me that his dragon healing hadn't cleared that up. "I deserved it."

"Well, whether you deserved it or not, violence is never the answer."

Broderick chuckled, and my dick stood at attention. I loved that sound. "I suppose you're right. But in this situation, I don't think anything would have snapped me out of my rant."

"It's okay," I said. "Actually, that's not even true. What you said is not okay at all. It's fine if you don't want a mate, but you don't really have to walk around bitching about it constantly. I don't have any more choice in this than you do."

"I know," Broderick said. "It's…," he paused. "It's not that I don't want a mate. I just don't want anything to happen to you. I've only been responsible for myself for the past two thousand years. It's hard to imagine sharing that with anyone else."

"That… sort of understandable," I said. Wolves longed to find their mates, they could barely contain themselves when they finally scented the person that the Fates had chosen just for them. But wolves, though long-lived because of their healing ability, were not immortal like dragons were; perhaps that made a difference.

"I don't think that you are weak, far from it. From what I understand from Frost, you've endured quite a lot in your life. And I'm sure growing up in a pack of wolves wasn't the easiest."

"No," I said. "But it was kind of fun."

"And you run fucking fast for a human."

I smiled. "Well, I didn't like being left out of the pack runs. So, I trained a lot, to keep up."

"I want you to stay here, where you can be protected by me and the other dragons. My friends and I will keep you safe from Molpe and that fucking vampire."

"I know," I said. "I don't want you to think that I came here hoping to be mated to you and make little dragon babies. I came here because my pack was running itself ragged trying to keep me safe, having extra guards on duty all the time, and it wasn't fair to them. Once the threat of Molpe and that vampire are gone, I don't have to be here anymore. And you and I can go our separate ways, okay?"

Broderick's jaw clenched, but he nodded. He looked like he wanted to say more but didn't.

"What is it?" I asked.

"Do you not want little dragon babies?"

I crossed my arms over my chest and stared at him. "Seems an odd question coming from a man who doesn't want to be mated."

He shrugged, unapologetically. "Just curious."

"I do want children," I said. "I always hoped that I would find myself a mate amongst the wolf pack and be changed into one of them. My mother had this vision the first time she saw me, that I would do something that would change the world as we know it. I don't know how accurate that is or what it even means, but I'd always hoped that it meant something cool was going to happen to me. Maybe it's this. Maybe it's having a dragon mate that doesn't want me. That's got to be unprecedented, right?"

Broderick growled. "How about we agree to play this whole mate thing by ear? See what happens while you're here?"

"Why? You were pretty clear on what you wanted." The last thing I wanted to do was delude myself into thinking that Broderick might change his mind, and I wasn't going to allow him to string me along either.

Broderick closed his eyes and pinched the bridge of his nose. "I'm sorry for what I said, I didn't mean it. I... I don't know what I want right now. It's all a little... sudden."

I gave him a sideways look. "We've known we were mates for two months now. If you need more time to figure out what you want, I can respect that. As long as you agree not to walk around bitching about the fact that your mate is a human."

"I can agree to that," Broderick said.

I hopped off the boulder. I'd reached my limit of emotional turmoil for the day. "I'll race you back to the house." I needed some space from him. Being this close, feeling his shoulder brush against mine as we spoke, nearly drove me mad.

Broderick chuckled. "I'm not much of a runner at this size. I'm more of a lineman, than a runningback."

"You fly. I'll run. I'll meet you there." I took off. Not because I was feeling overly playful, but because I didn't know how much longer I could be in Broderick's presence, alone, without doing something stupid like begging him to mate me, care for me, love me like I'd seen other mates do.

I took off at a full sprint, running back toward the house. Another advantage to growing up with a bunch of wolves who like to roam around the forest, you learn to have a good sense of direction or you got lost a lot.

I arrived back at the house and let myself in the back door. It would be quite the adjustment to get used to this huge house when I was used to living in what essentially equated to cabins at the wolf pack compound. A one room house with a small kitchenette and a private bathroom. We had a common area at the Alpha's house, where we had most of our meals and access to a larger kitchen. Dragon Headquarters was practically a mansion, three stories, a suite for each of the dragons, a huge library and Frost had even mentioned a home theater area.

"Oh, thank god."

I turned and found Flint standing there.

"I found him!" He called out. He grabbed my hand and pulled me toward the kitchen. "Jericho was just about to go after you."

When I got into the kitchen, Broderick was already standing there, Jericho next to him, looking like he was going to tear out his throat.

"I did not bring him here so that he would be made fun of and treated poorly." Jericho glared daggers at Broderick, who simply crossed his arms. "I'm taking him home. We'll figure out a way to keep him safe. At the very least, we'll treat him a hell of a lot better than you will."

"Jericho," I said. "I can't go home now, you've said so yourself. Those reasons haven't changed."

"What? After what this stupid brute said?"

I placed a hand on Jericho's shoulder. "Broderick promised not to be an asshole. It'll be fine."

Leonidas let out a low whistle. "I'd love to know how you got him to agree to that. We've been trying for the last century or so."

Broderick flipped him the bird.

"Broderick and I will just stay away from each other," I said. "It shouldn't be that difficult. This house is huge. As long as I have a place to do my artwork, I'll be just fine. Besides, it will be nice to spend some time with Frost and Crispin. You need to focus on Cody." That got through to him.

Jericho's jaw clenched. "Alright. Call me if anything changes, okay? I'll be here faster than you can pack your bag."

"I know you will," I said, and I stepped into his arms for a hug. "You're probably the best wolf brother in the entire world."

He snorted. "No 'probably' about it. I am the best." He hugged me close to him. "Stay safe, okay?"

"I will." Though we weren't brothers by blood, Jericho had come to mean more to me than anyone in the world. Well, him and Frost. I knew he would do whatever he could to keep me safe.

A low growl had me stepping out of Jericho's embrace and looking around the room. I found Broderick standing against the wall, hands clenched at his sides, his face twisted in a snarl.

"Calm down," I said. "He's my brother. Besides, you don't want a mate, remember?"

He softened at that and looked away,

Jericho stepped toward him until they were standing chest to chest. "If anything happens to my brother while he is under your care, last stone dragon or not, I will come out here, hunt you down, and turn your hide into snakeskin boots."

"I'm a dragon, not a snake."

"You're a reptile. And I'll make a belt to match."

"His scales really aren't your color, Jericho," I said. The rest of the room chuckled. "Besides, you won't need to. Nothing is going to happen to me."

Jericho nodded. He and Armant stepped outside. I watched from the window as Armant shifted and Jericho climbed onto his back. The two took off.

I stared into the sky until I couldn't see them anymore.

A hand rested on my shoulder and I leaned into it. I turned hoping to find my mate there, but I found the next best thing instead—Frost.

"C'mon. I'll show you to your room."

***

Frost led me up the stairs and down a series of hallways, until we stood outside a single wood door. He pointed toward the end of the hall. "Those are Broderick's rooms, just in case you wanted to know. And across the hall is the game room I showed you the last time you were here." He pushed the door open and we walked in.

The room was simple, but way more extravagant that I was used to. There was a stark white, five-drawer dresser, a double bed and a nightstand. The pale green walls reflected the sunlight from the east window.

"We don't really have guest rooms, so we ordered all this stuff new. Hope you don't mind."

"Not at all," I said. "Its wonderful. Thank you. I'm sorry you had to go through all that trouble."

He waved his hand in the air. "Besides a newborn, I'm not overly busy. And I can order items online while holding Crispin. I'm great at multi-tasking."

I placed my duffel bag that held the extent of the items I'd brought with me on the green and beige bedspread. We had already dropped off my tools in the garage for me to set up there so that I could continue my work while living here. Frost had assured me that none of the dragons would mind if I used the space.

"I'm really glad you're here," Frost said.

I smiled. "Me too. It'll be nice to hang out. I'd imagine you guys get a little bored out here. Not much to do."

Frost laughed. "Yeah, Flint and I have been talking to Leonidas and Gale about that, and they've agreed that we can leave the property more often. After all, the kids are going to need exposure to the outside world sooner or later. I'm not going to homeschool them."

"Yeah, I don't really envy that challenge of trying to figure out how to put a dragon child in preschool." I supposed that was one bright side to having a mate who wasn't interested in me.

"Hey," Frost said as he laid a hand on my shoulder. "You just might have to think about that too. If you and Broderick ever mate."

"I doubt that's going to happen." I sat on the bed, then sunk back into the mattress. "He's made his stance quite clear. I would love to be in a relationship, especially one with my fated mate. There's nothing like it in the world, I'm told. But, I'm not going to force him into anything. I'd rather he want me for me, not because the Fates decide."

Frost kneeled on the bed and looked down at me. "I think he'll come around eventually. His bark is worse than his bite."

I snorted. "I hope so, but I won't be holding my breath. I don't really need to set myself up for any disappointment."

Chapter Four

Mason

After a week at Dragon Headquarters, I still hadn't quite settled. The bed was comfortable, and I liked my room. But more often than not, I found myself lying awake at night staring at the ceiling. If it got too awful, I would venture out and roam the hallways, pick up a few books in the library and curl up in Broderick's chair in the game room. I hadn't been able to create any new art since being here. I had an adequate setup in the garage, a few pieces of stone ready to be carved, and plenty of time on my hands. But no ideas came to mind.

I sat at the kitchen table, sketch book in hand, but it remained blank.

Flint entered the room and I snapped out of my daze. "Are you coming with us to the zoo?" He asked.

I perked up at that. "We're leaving the property?"

"Yeah," Flint said. "I finally got Leo to agree. Frost got Gale on board, and we're heading off to the zoo. You want to go?"

"Yeah," I said. I closed my sketchbook and tossed my pencil down. Maybe I would find some inspiration there. "You know, your kids are probably going to sleep through the whole thing, right?"

"Yeah, yeah," Flint waved his hand in the air. "Keegan's not even one yet. And Crispin is just shy of three months. But getting them out and about is still important, exposure to life and all that. Plus, I've been holed up in this house for almost a year. It's time that I see people again. I hope I remember how to act in public."

I laughed at that. "Don't take your cues from me. I've never been sure of how to act. I grew up with a wolf pack, remember?"

"Well, good. We can all look weird together."

"Just don't draw too much attention to us." Leonidas came into the room. He wrapped his hands around his mate's waist and kissed his neck.

My heart tugged at the sight. I longed for a connection like that. Wanted my mate to come up behind me, touch me and kiss me like I mattered to him. Like I was the most important thing in the world. Instead, I'd barely even seen Broderick around the house. He seemed to steer clear of me as much as he possibly could.

Just then, Broderick stormed into the room. *Speak of the devil,* I thought to myself.

"What are you all up to?"

Leonidas grinned as he looked at him. "Apparently, we're taking a trip to the zoo. Flint and Frost think the kids will enjoy it."

Broderick snorted. "The kids won't know they're at the zoo."

"That's what I said, but we're going anyway," I chimed in.

Broderick spun to face me. "You can't go anywhere."

I raised an eyebrow. "Excuse me? I can do whatever I damn well please."

"It's too dangerous." He stepped closer to me, invading my space. "You need to stay here."

I stood tall, refusing to back down. I knew Broderick was used to people bending to his will due to his size, but I had family members that regularly turned into wolves, his chest thumping didn't faze me. "Gale and Leonidas will be there. It will be fine."

"And they can be there to protect their own mates. You need to stay here."

"Yeah, you keep saying that, but you're not going to change my mind. I'm going." I put my hands on my hips.

"Fine," he said. "Then I'm going too."

He took a step back from me, and the reality of the situation hit. I'd be spending the day with my mate.

***

At the zoo, Flint and Leonidas pushed Keegan in a stroller that seemed way too big and complicated for one baby. Frost wore some sort of baby carrying contraption that strapped Crispin against his chest. The little guy slept soundly as we walked from exhibit to exhibit.

Gale and Leonidas didn't let their mates too far out of their sight. They stayed pretty well plastered to their side the entire time we were out.

Broderick walked beside me. He paid no attention to the animals, always looking at the people at the zoo. Sizing all of them up, I supposed. "Would you calm down?" I said. "You're making it look like you're my bodyguard."

"Right now, I am," he said. "I promised Jericho that nothing would happen to you."

I rolled my eyes. "Fine," I said. I pulled out my phone and snapped a few pictures of the wolves in the exhibit. "They're a lot smaller than the ones back home," I said.

Finally, he looked at the animals instead of the people around us and he made a small noise.

I snuck a glance at him. He had a slight smile tugging at his lips. "Did you just laugh at that?" I said.

He all out smiled. "Yeah," he said. "I did."

"Damn. It wasn't even that funny." I walked on, coming up to the big cats.

The lion roared as we walked up to its enclosure. "Wow," I said. "It's probably not every day the visitors at the zoo get to see that."

"No, I suppose not." Broderick crossed his arms and looked in at the big animal. Suddenly, the lion leaped from its perch and walked right up to the glass, staring at Broderick. Nose to nose.

My eyes widened, and I sucked in a breath. "What's it doing?" I said.

"I think it senses another predator. One it doesn't quite recognize." He never looked away from the big cat.

"Well, you're kind of making a scene," I said.

Other people at the zoo started crowding around, impressed at the lion looking so lively and close.

"Look away from it," I whispered.

A low growl sounded in Broderick's throat.

"Oh, for christ's sake," I said. "This is no time to play 'Who's the bigger predator.' Let it win this round, I assure you, you can take it in a fight." I linked my arm around Broderick's and tugged him away.

Finally, Broderick dropped his stare and turned away from the beast. It roared, showing off its strength and Broderick hesitated, but I pulled him along.

"See? Was that so hard?"

He shrugged. "A little damaging to the ego, but I suppose I'll live this time."

I laughed as we walked, our arms remained linked for the rest of the visit.

Chapter Five

Broderick

The zoo had proved to be more fun than I ever would have guessed. I couldn't remember a time when I been around so many other people. When was the last time I did anything for fun like that? I couldn't remember that either.

Sure, I went out to the bar with my coworkers after a long day in the sun. But that didn't compare at all to the time I'd spent at the zoo with my mate. For a moment, I could picture us there with our child, running from exhibit to exhibit, showing them the animals. Hell, I'd even enjoyed staring down the lion, though Mason made me walk away from it, which wounded my dragon's pride. The human side of me knew that I couldn't get into a pissing match with another predator based on pride alone.

I had to walk away because of the other humans in the area, but I knew that my dragon could snap the lion in two if we met in the wild.

When we got back to the house, both kids were sleeping so Frost, Gale, Flint and Leonidas disappeared into the house, mumbling something about sleeping while the babies slept.

Mason and I stood outside. He glanced between the garage and the house.

"Thinking about getting some work done?" I asked.

He shrugged. "I'm not feeling overly inspired these days. All of my ideas have run dry since I've been here."

"Oh," I said. Not sure exactly how to respond. I knew my mate was talented, I'd seen his pieces, pictures of them online at least. The dragon carving that Frost had gotten as a gift from Mason was exquisite.

"Want to go flying?" I blurted out.

He turned around and looked at me. "With you?"

"I don't see any other dragons out here," I said.

He bit his lip and shifted his weight from one foot to the other.

I held up my hands. "No strings attached. Just go for quick flight around the property. I promise I won't let anything happen to you."

"I know," he said. "It's just, you've been avoiding me for a week now."

"Well, I figured you could use your space."

He chewed his lip some more. "I'm not the one who wants space, Broderick." My name on his lips went straight to my cock.

"Do you want to go flying or not?" I asked.

"I do."

"Let's go." I started stripping off my clothes, tossing them on to the ground. He continued to stare at me, his gaze never leaving my body and I deliberately slowed my movements.

He rolled his eyes. "I don't have all day, you know."

"Oh, yeah? You've got some pressing business to attend to?"

He stomped his foot. "You know, you don't have to be such an asshole."

"It's in my nature, mate. Sorry." There was no apology in my voice.

He turned to leave, and I thought maybe I'd lost him, so I quickly transformed into my dragon, hoping the abrupt change would stop him in his tracks. It did. I towered over him. He looked tiny compared to my huge brute of a dragon.

"Holy shit," he said. "You're huge."

I rumbled at that.

He laughed. "I'm sure you hear that all the time."

I held out one arm and he took a confident step forward without hesitation, which made my dragon preen. Our mate felt safe with us. He wasn't scared at all. Once he climbed into my outstretched hand, I was able to help him onto my back and he settled between my wings.

I wish I'd been able to give him a fair warning that I'd be taking off, but I didn't think to inform him prior to switching over. Once I knew he held on tight, I launched into the air. He let out a shrill of surprise, but there was no fear. I flapped my wings lifting higher into the air until I caught an air pocket and coasted.

"This is amazing!"

I smiled inwardly. Making my mate happy, hearing his joy, feeling his joy through our incomplete bond was like nothing I'd ever experienced before. And I wanted more of it. Being with him today, experiencing the zoo together made me realize how it could be if we were together for real. I flew for a while, not wanting the time I spent with him to end, not wanting to go back to my human form where I would say stupid, rude things that would piss him off and push him away. As a dragon I didn't think logically about having a mate. I didn't think about the loss, about what it would feel like if Mason was taken from me.

Although I knew it wasn't fair to him to run so hot and cold each day. It had to be confusing and annoying. My dragon didn't care.

After flying for a while, Mason shifted on my back. He lay down, sprawling out completely between my wings. As gently as I could, I touched down and he slid off me.

"Wow," he said, wobbling a bit as he tried to walk. "That was amazing."

We'd landed in my favorite clearing, the place where I'd found him just a week ago, when he'd run off after I said those horrible things. I transformed back to my human self.

Mason rested on a rock and I sat next to him.

"Is this your clearing?" he asked.

"Yeah," I said. "I had the rocks brought in. My dragon sometimes likes to lay down on them, and sleep. I once spent a whole a week camped out here, just sleeping on the rocks."

"Really?" He asked. "A whole week just sleeping?"

I shrugged. "Yeah, when you have all the time in the world at your disposal and no one to share it with…"

"I get that," he said. "Can't quite imagine it, but I sort of understand." He lay back and rested his hands behind his head, staring at the sky.

I looked down at him. His eyes were closed, his hands behind his head, completely relaxed, breathtaking. Before I could think better of it, I leaned down and kissed his lips. He sucked in a breath of surprise, but then kissed me back. His hand going around my neck, holding me close to him. I wanted a better angle, and I didn't want to crush him. So, I hoisted him into the air until he straddled my lap, deepening the kiss. My tongue seeking entrance into his mouth, stroking his tongue, drawing a moan from him.

His taste was something I'd never forget, something I wanted to experience every day for the rest of my life. Was it like this for all mates? If so, I could definitely see the appeal.

My hand trailed down his stomach, under his shirt and I found the waist of his jeans. I stilled, waiting for permission. Mason bucked his hips.

"Please. Touch me," he moaned.

That was all I needed to hear.

I slipped my hand inside, tugging at the pants with my other hand to get them off him.

My cock leaked already, and I hadn't even laid a hand on myself.

I lifted away from his lips and he whimpered. I winked at him and whirled us around, so that I stood, and he lay back on the rocks again. Then I slid down his body. I took his hardened cock into my hand, pumped it a few times, then I stuck my tongue out to catch the bead of cum leaking from the tip.

He tasted better than the finest wine. My eyes rolled into the back of my head. I had to have more of him. All at once I took him completely into my mouth. Licking, sucking, drawing pleasure as well as giving it.

Mason's hand went to the back of my head and he laced his fingers through my hair.

I rolled his balls in my hand, loving the feel of them, the weight of them.

I'd never bothered giving blow jobs to my lovers before, but this was different. Mason was different. I was made for him, and he for me. There would be no more lovers for either of us.

"Broderick." His breath came in short, hard pants and I knew it wouldn't be much longer.

I doubled down, bobbing up and down the length of him, my cheeks hollowing as I sucked him down.

The first shot of cum hit the back of my throat and his hips jerked, pushing him deeper into my mouth. I loved it. My mate fucked my face and I couldn't get enough. His cum filled my mouth, and I swallowed as much of it as I could, until it was too much, and it leaked from my mouth.

I sat back, wiped off my chin, and grinned at him.

He lay on the rock, breathing heavily, his cock softening against his exposed thigh.

I climbed up next to him and pulled him against me.

"That was amazing," he said.

I chuckled. "I'm glad you liked it."

He sighed against my chest and snuggled closer. We lay like that for a while afterward. Our fingers laced together as we stared up at the sky. I asked him about his family, and he told me about the mischief he and Jericho had gotten into when they were younger, about how he'd gotten into stone carving, and the odd jobs he'd done around the pack compound. I was content to stay there forever next to my mate, hearing him talk about his life, his hopes, his dreams, his artwork.

Here in the clearing, I could ignore the threat of the outside world. Ignore the fact that at any given moment my mate could be ripped from my arms and taken from me, that any child we created would be in danger. But then Mason's stomach rumbled, indicating to me that my mate needed sustenance.

I sat up. "Hungry?"

He smiled. "A little bit."

"C'mon," I said. "Let's get you to the kitchen."

I took a step back from him and transformed into my dragon. He laid a hand on my scales, caressing my neck.

"You're absolutely gorgeous," he said.

I let out a roar and he jumped. "That's quite impressive as well," he said.

I preened at the compliment. I helped him onto my back and took off. I didn't bother playing around this time, I went straight for the house.

It was almost completely dark by the time we got back, so I landed and helped Mason off my back, transforming quickly into my human form. I put my clothes back on and grabbed Mason's hand, leading him into the house to the kitchen where I could make sure he had his fill of food before taking him up to my room.

Unfortunately, we weren't alone in our evening snack endeavors. We found the entire household in the kitchen, huddled around a laptop.

"What's going on?" Mason asked.

"Oh, nothing. Just me being a genius," Flint said.

I cocked an eyebrow at that. "Oh, really? That'll be new and different."

Flint stuck his tongue out at me. Leonidas pulled him back onto his lap. "We put some of Flint's computer skills to use. He had the brilliant idea of putting together a composite image of the vampire to see if we could find someone who recognizes him. As of right now we know absolutely nothing about him. Not even his name. We figured Valerie could take this around and see if anyone has heard of him."

"Awesome. Like a police sketch artist." I pulled open the fridge, grabbed a half full pizza box, and looked at Mason. "You like cold pizza?"

He grinned. "Yeah, it's the best."

I winked. "I agree." I intended to take the pizza back to my suite with me and Mason as well, see if we couldn't pick up where we left off once his stomach was full.

"Mason, you haven't seen the vampire yet. Here. This is who we're looking for." Frost handed Mason a sheet of paper.

I recognized the murderous face immediately. "That's damn good work, Flint. I'm impressed. Looks just like him."

"Peter," Mason whispered, so quiet I almost didn't hear it.

"What?" I asked.

Mason looked up, looking around at everyone frantically. "This is the vampire?" He said.

"Yeah. Do you recognize him?" Gale asked.

I took a step toward Mason. My heart rate increased. "You know him?" I growled. I already knew the answer, recognition firing in Mason's eyes.

"Yes," Mason said. "He's a regular at the shop back home. He—he's one of my best customers."

We all stood stunned, looking at him.

"How long has he been a customer?" Gale asked slowly.

"Just a couple of months. I saw him the first time after I came back from being here, when we returned home with Cody."

After he met me. I crumpled the pizza box that I held in my hands.

"How could he possibly know about Mason? No one beyond this property knows about Mason being my mate. How could he have found him?" My breath came in short pants and the edges of my vision blurred, kicking my anger up another notch.

Gale and Leonidas exchanged a look.

"How?" I roared.

"We don't know," Gale said.

"Did you talk to him a lot?" Frost asked as he grabbed Mason's hand and guided him to the table to sit. "What do you know about him? What can you tell us?"

Confusion clouded my mate's face. He wouldn't meet my gaze. "Not much. He came in a few times. He bought a few of my pieces. He was friendly, he—" Mason bit his lip.

"What?" I said. I slammed my fist on the counter. "Tell me."

"Back off, Broderick," Frost said. "You being an asshole isn't going to help."

I gripped the edge of the counter top to ground myself and waited for my mate to speak.

"He was friendly. He always wore thick cologne, probably to mask his scent, now that I think about it. There's no way that he could be walking around a town full of wolves and not have anyone notice. He only came in a few times, but he would call and ask about my new pieces and when I would be working, at least once a week. I didn't think anything of it." Mason snuck a glance at me before he continued. "I saw him the last day I was there, when I went to pick up my tools. He—he gave me his number, and he kissed me on the cheek, told me that he would miss me, and he'd keep in touch."

The granite countertop snapped under the force of my hold.

"Ignore him," Frost said. "What more can you tell us?"

"That's it," Mason said. "I've texted him a few times since I've been here, but not much."

"Why would you give him your number?" I roared.

Mason glared. "He was nice to me, alright? He asked for it and I gave it to him. A lot of my clients have my number. How the fuck was I supposed to know that he was a vampire? I'm just a weak, fragile human, remember? Aside from the creepy huge amulet he wore and the overused cologne, he was completely normal."

"He wore an amulet?" Leonidas asked. "What did it look like?"

Mason shrugged. "I don't know, I only saw it once. But he seemed to try and cover it up, like he didn't want me to know he had it. That's the only thing that sticks out about him."

"Can you describe it for me?" Flint asked.

Mason nodded. "I can draw it for you if you want."

"That would be perfect. We can send it to Armant and Valerie, see what they know about it. It could be something. Could be nothing."

Unable to hear any more so I left the room. Angry at the vampire for getting anywhere near my mate. I couldn't wait for the day that I would tear his throat out and burn him alive. But mostly I was angry at myself for letting my mate be in that situation for two months. That vampire had free access to Mason during that time because I was busy having my head stuck in my ass. I was lucky that he hadn't done anything then.

What the hell was he waiting for? How could he possibly know that Mason was my mate?

I grabbed a bottle of whiskey from the liquor cabinet and went outside to the deck. I sat on a bench, staring off into the distance.

How was I going to fix this?

It wasn't that long ago that I was positive that I didn't want a mate, didn't want to worry about a mate, worry about the loss. But now getting a taste of him, literally, I realized there was so much more to having a mate. I'd begun to see that the benefits just might outweigh the risks. Question was, did I really think I could go through with it? Open myself up to that kind of pain?

Merek sat down in the chair beside me.

"Want to talk about it?" He asked.

"Not particularly." I took a swig of the whiskey, then handed it to him.

He shook his head. "That's all you, man. I don't have any sorrows to drown just yet."

I snorted. "Well, I'm sure when you find your mate, you'll have plenty of anxiety to go along with it."

"Is that what this is about?" He said. "You think having a mate is too tough, so you want to just not claim him? Push him away?"

"I don't know. That's how I felt at first, but the more time I spend with him…" I trailed off, he got the idea, I didn't need to continue.

"I'd give anything to find my mate right now," Merek said quietly.

"You will in due time, I'm sure."

"Before or after the vampire or Molpe gets him?"

I put a hand on his shoulder. "We won't let that happen."

"Well, you already let your mate nearly slip through your fingers."

My dragon roared at that. "I have not," I said indignantly. "Mason is mine."

"Then act like it," Merek said. "You should be comforting him right now. At the very least, listen to what he has to say. Instead, you stormed out like a petulant child, just like you do every time he's around. You storm out of the room and avoid him."

I wanted to tell him to mind his own damn business and leave me the fuck alone. What did he know? But I knew that wasn't fair. My behavior was exactly as he'd described. All of us knew loss. I was the only weak one who couldn't seem to handle it after two thousand years.

"What if I lose him?" I said quietly. "What if I can't protect him? I couldn't protect my brothers or their mates from the war all those years ago. Stone dragons—the brutes, the heavy lifters of the dragon species were the first recruits, and the biggest casualties. Nothing I did or said convinced my family not to fight. I couldn't save them. Why would this be any different? The black dragons, the jewel dragons, you all were the masterminds. You played your part, and it was a big part, but you weren't on the front lines."

"No," Merek said. "We weren't. But they're all dead just the same. We were chosen to stay because we didn't believe that we were superior simply because we were dragons. And now after all these years, the Fates have given us our mates, allowed us to continue the dragon species. And you want to throw all that away because you're afraid that you might lose him? That's fucking stupid, Broderick. You think that Gale and Leonidas regret having their mates? You've seen them with Frost and Flint, and those two babies. How can you not want that?"

"I do. More than anything. But I don't want to lose him."

Merek grabbed the bottle from me and took a swig. "Well, brother, you might not need to worry about that too much longer. You've caused irreparable damage at this point."

I took the bottle back from him and finished it. I'd need several more swigs if I actually wanted to get a buzz. I hoped Merek was wrong, but I couldn't help but wonder. I stood and started back towards the house.

"Where are you going?" he said.

"I'm going to fix this."

***

I paced around my room, rehearsing in my head what I could say to Mason to help him to understand and forgive me for the things that I'd done in pushing him away. I'd start with 'I'm sorry, and I promise to do better,' and I hoped to hell that that would at least get him to listen to me. Then I'd explain about my family.

I stood in front of my door, took a deep breath, and opened it, ready to march out and track down Mason, either in his room or camped out in the game room. Instead, I found him standing just outside my door, hand raised ready to knock. The rehearsed speech I had in my head lost in my confusion.

"Hi," I said, taken aback at seeing him standing in front of me.

"Hi," he said.

"I'm sorry," I said. "Why don't you come in?"

He looked taken aback at that. "Really?"

"Yeah," I said.

He stepped into my room. It was similar in size to the other guy's suites, only mine was plain. I preferred earthy tones. The walls were beige, the carpet was beige, pretty much everything was some shade of beige.

"I'm not going to apologize for talking to Peter," Mason said. "I had no way of knowing what he was. I am sorry that he kissed me."

My blood boiled at that, knowing that the vampire had laid hands on my mate.

"It's not your fault," I said. "I understand you had no way of knowing. I'm not mad at you about that. I'm not mad at you at all. That damn vampire…" I took a deep breath. Now, or never. Time for me to fully come clean in order for my mate and I to move forward.

My gaze locked with his. "I'm terrified, Mason," I said.

He cocked his head to the side and took a step toward me. "What do you mean? Of what?"

"I'm terrified of losing you, of losing any children that we may have."

His brow furrowed in genuine confusion. "Why would you lose me? Mates can't leave each other, it's just not possible. Once you're bonded, you're bonded for life," he said.

"That's just it, it's for life and in my experience, the lives of people I love end. I lose them. Two thousand years ago, before the war, before dragons were wiped from the Earth. I had four brothers and my two dads. We all worked together in the mines. Being stone dragons, that was kind of our thing. Manual labor. It's why I still do construction jobs to this day. The others have all amassed their fortunes with businesses of some sort. I've never owned a business in my life. I've amassed a fortune via good investments, but I've still mostly just done manual labor my entire life. It's what stone dragons are good for."

I ran a hand through my hair.

Mason opened his mouth to say something, but I stopped him. I needed to get this out.

"My brother, Carrik, was one of the first recruited for the army. He was bigger than me, if you can imagine that. Stronger than me too. Younger, though, and more hot-headed. He had a mate. They were young, even in human years. But they were so in love. I was envious of him having found his mate so early in life, while I still searched for mine. I tried to talk him out of helping with the war effort, but he didn't listen to me. It paid well, and he couldn't imagine that the dragons would lose. The invincibility of youth and all that."

Mason wrapped his arms around my waist and hugged me tight. I appreciated the comfort.

"He left for training. His mate was a month along with their first child. The house was attacked. I'm not even sure by who. They used something that made it difficult to shift, we couldn't concentrate. I was knocked unconscious. I don't know why I was left alive. When I came to, Carrick was there, holding his dead mate in his arms, sobbing." I closed my eyes. It'd been so long since I'd even thought about that day. But the emotion was still raw within me.

"Carrick never recovered. He could never call forth his dragon after that. He didn't speak, didn't eat. The next time we were attacked, he didn't fight back. It wasn't long after that the Fates intervened, and the war came to an end."

"I'm not going anywhere." Mason stepped back and raised a hand to cup my cheek, forcing me to meet his gaze. "I'm just as scared as you are. I'm *human* living amongst mythical creatures. And despite the fact that I've lived amongst them my entire life, I still can't shake the inadequacies I feel sometimes. But human or not, I know that this is right. We're mates. We can't be without each other, we can't fight it. And I don't want to."

I leaned forward and connected my forehead with his. "You're not *just* anything. You're an amazing, gorgeous, sweet man. And I can't believe how lucky I am to call you mate."

Mason smiled. "It's about time you realized. Show me."

I connected my lips with his crashing down on him hard. He gave back just as good as he got, wrapping his arms around my neck, and hooking one leg around my hip, climbing me like a polecat.

I hoisted him in the air, and carried him to the bed. I laid him down softly, without ever lifting my lips from his. I ripped off his pants and shirt, then made quick work of my own clothes, tossing them to the floor to be taken care of later, if we ever came up for air and out of this bed.

His hands were everywhere, caressing my chest, rubbing down my biceps. His fingertips trailed over my nipples. My cock jutted out from my body, already leaking pre-cum.

"Are you sure about this?"

"Yes," he said. "Claim me. Make me yours. Knot me, like I've heard the omega's talk about. I want to know what that feels like."

My dragon roared, ready to take our mate hard and fast, again and again. But I slowed myself down. "Have you…?" I trailed off.

Mason pushed me back a bit so that our eyes met. "No," he said. "I've always waited for my mate. Waited for you."

My control nearly slipped just then, and I groaned, crashing my lips down on his again. My fingers went to his entrance, probing gently. His body leaked slick as it prepared itself for me. I easily slipped in two digits, scissoring them to stretch the ring of muscle. He bucked his hips, welcoming the intrusion.

"Oh fuck," he said.

I kissed his neck, sucking, licking, tasting as much of him as I could.
- When I removed my fingers, Mason whimpered. I lined my cock up to his entrance and pushed in slowly. His body opened for me, and I slid in like I belonged there.

Mason groaned when I bottomed out and pulled back again. With each thrust of my hips, his cries of pleasure rose higher and higher. I pumped his cock and before too long, he shot his load between us, pearly white cum landing on his chest.

The sight threw me over the edge and I came inside him, burying my seed deep within my mate.

My cock swelled, and Mason writhed beneath me. More cum shot from his dick.

"Oh, god. Broderick!"

My knot expanded against the walls of his channel and Mason's eyes rolled back. "Oh fuck. It's too good. I can't take it."

I captured his lips with mine, silencing his screams that I was sure had reached the other rooms by now. We kissed slowly, and our breathing returned to normal. My knot still held, so I rolled over until Mason lay on top of me, still connected. I stroked his head, whispering to him, telling him how perfect, wonderful, and amazing he was.

When my knot finally deflated, and I was able to slip out of him, he slept. I gently moved him off me and got us cleaned up, then climbed back into bed with him.

My mate. In my bed. It was perfect.

He snuggled against me as I pulled the cover over us.

"Tell me about your brothers. All of them, before the war," Mason said sleepily.

"I'm not even sure where to start."

"At the beginning."

Chapter Six

Mason

The ringing of my phone broke my concentration and I put down the dragon carving I was working on, created in the likeness of my own mate. It would be a piece that I would keep for myself, not for sale.

Since Broderick had claimed me, we barely spent any time outside of our bedroom. But when we did come up for air, I was able to work on my art again. My muse had returned. Already, I had shipped pieces back home to sell at the shop and listed a few online. I had another stack of packages ready to take to the post office today, as long as Broderick would let me go. Of course, he would insist on going with me, which was perfectly fine, since I preferred to be near him anyway.

Even now, as I worked on my carvings in the garage, he was just outside in the backyard measuring and planning where he would be building a playset for all the kids. I'd told him that he could buy premade sets online, but he'd scoffed at the idea, saying that he would build a custom playset fit for dragons. I hadn't yet seen the sketches he'd put together for what he was planning, but already I was terrified of what he would come up with.

I picked up my phone, checked my notifications; I'd gotten a text alert saying that the new tools I'd ordered online had arrived. I checked the time and I had missed the outgoing post for today. Time had gotten away from me this morning after Broderick and I had crawled out of bed. If I didn't go to the post office now, I'd have to wait until tomorrow.

I sat my tools down and made my way outside. Broderick stood, hammer in hand, staking out the spot he planned to use for the playset.

"That looks huge."

Broderick turned to me and smiled. "It's thirty feet squared."

"Just how big of a sandbox do you think these kids need?"

Broderick shrugged. "We have all this room. We might as well use it."

"Yeah, but this might be overkill, don't you think?"

"Once the kids start shifting, they'll need plenty of space to play," he countered.

Oh, christ. I didn't even want to think about what would happen when the babies started shifting. Just the other day Keegan had sneezed, and smoke had come out of his ears, which had sent Flint into a frenzy. Every room now had a fire extinguisher mounted on the wall, just in case.

"My packages arrived in town. Want to go to the post office real quick?"

Broderick tossed his hammer down and wrapped his arms around my waist pulling me against him. "Do we have time for a quickie first?"

I moaned and ground my hips against his. "I wish we did, but unfortunately, if we don't leave now we'll miss closing and we won't be able to go until tomorrow. And tomorrow I'd like to spend the entire day in bed with you."

"That's what I wanted to do today, but you insisted on getting out of bed." He kissed my neck and I clutched at his shoulders.

"I promise I'll make it up to you if we go right now."

He stepped back, and I staggered without him there to support me.

"Alright, I suppose. We'll swing by the lumberyard and I'll pick up the supplies I need for this." He handed me his sketchbook and my eyes widened.

"Jesus," I said. "That's massive. That's not even a swing set. It's an entire play yard."

He'd drawn a castle structure, with two towers, connected by a rope bridge, and two slides down the center. "Is that a working drawbridge?"

"Yeah," he said. "I thought that would be fun. You can turn this wheel here," he pointed to the page, "and lift the bridge up and down."

"Oh, for god's sake," I said. "You think that's going to be safe?"

He shrugged. "They're dragon babies. Tough little boys. They can handle it."

"Sure. But maybe you should get this idea approved by Flint and Frost first."

"I talked to Leonidas and Gale about it yesterday and they said it was fine."

"If you say so."

He grabbed my hand and the two of us walked to his truck. We stopped in the garage and Broderick effortlessly picked up the stack of packages I had and placed them in the bed of his truck.

I hoisted myself into the passenger seat while he took his place in the driver's side.

"Alright, if we're leaving the property, you remember the rules?"

I rolled my eyes. "Yes, I remember the rules. My cell phone is in my pocket. I have my SOS button thing that Merek insisted we carry, and I will not, under any circumstances, leave your side. At any point, if something happens and we are separated, I'm to send text messages and phone calls to anybody I can and scream very, very loudly."

I recited the plan we'd put together. Flint, Frost, and I had the emergency protocol drilled into our heads. We wanted to be prepared for the next time that Peter and Molpe struck. So, far we'd hit dead end after dead end on finding out more information about Peter. Armant had been traveling around the country talking with different vampire covens to find out where Peter might be from and what his deal was.

Broderick seemed satisfied by me reciting the rules, because he pressed the button to open the garage door and drove out.

I held his hand throughout the drive to town, enjoying the scenery.

***

Once delivered everything to the post office, Broderick and I walked out of the building hand in hand, swinging our arms. Carefree, like we didn't have a worry in the world.

"Hey, you know what we should do before we go get the lumber?

"What?"

"Get ice cream." I spun around so that I was holding both of his hands and walking backwards. "Come on. It'll be fun. I saw a place on our way into town."

"I'm not a big ice cream guy," he said. "Do you think they have any real food there? I could go for a burger."

"We just had lunch," I said. The thought of a burger turned my stomach. I put a hand on my stomach.

Broderick narrowed his eyes at me. "Maybe ice cream isn't a good idea for you either."

"No, ice cream sounds delicious, burgers sound gross."

He chuckled. "Alright, we'll get ice cream."

Just as I was about to turn around and walk forward again, I felt a presence behind me and Broderick immediately pulled me to his side, pushing me behind him. He growled, low in his throat.

Peter stood before us. My blood ran cold and panic set in.

"What are you doing here?" I said.

"Oh, I just came in to check on the dragon mates, see how they're doing." Peter looked from Broderick and then back to me. "Molpe and I were just arguing the other day whether or not you'd actually mate with this brute. Seems I was wrong. You've disappointed me, Mason."

I opened my mouth to shout at him, to tell him he knew nothing of me and Broderick, but Broderick spoke first.

"Get the fuck away from my mate, vampire, before I tear you limb from limb."

Peter laughed out loud and maniacally. "You'd have to catch me first."

Broderick lunged, and Peter disappeared, only to reappear again behind us.

I looked around the street nervously. Thankfully, it didn't appear that anyone was taking any notice of us. Another trick of his, perhaps? It seemed as though his powers were limitless. How in the hell were we going to fight against that?

"Leave us alone, Peter." I grabbed Broderick's hand, pulling him toward the car. The only way we were going to be safe was if we got back to headquarters.

"Come on, Mason. You know you can do better than that dragon. Just say the word and I'll take you for my own mate. You could live an eternal life just like me, as a vampire."

The thought of drinking blood for the rest of my life really made my stomach roll, and I held a hand over my stomach again, the blood draining from my face.

Peter's eyes widened, like he just realized something. "Ah, I see," Peter said. "So, the prophecy is going to come to fruition. The stone dragon's mate carries a baby."

That was news to me. Broderick stiffened beside me, wrapping his arms around me protectively. "Leave vampire."

"Oh," Peter said. "You two didn't know yet." He folded his hands together. "I'm delighted to inform you that you two are going to be parents or a least Mason will. If I have anything to say about it, you'll be long gone before the baby gets here." Peter reached a hand out and tried to stroke my face, but I flinched away from him, curling in next to Broderick. "I'll be seeing you, Mason. Don't worry, you and I can raise your child together." And then suddenly, he was gone.

"Motherfucker." Broderick's fists clenched to his side.

"Come on." I tugged his arm. "Let's go home. We need to figure out how to stop this guy."

***

When we got back to the house, Broderick hopped out of the truck, ran to the other side, and lifted me out before I could even open my own door. He cradled me against him, walking into the house with purpose.

"I can walk," I said.

"I know," he said curtly. "But I'm not putting you down ever."

"That seems like it might get a little tiresome, especially as I get bigger." I smiled.

His face went stark white and a sweat broke out on his forehead.

I wiggled out of his arms and stood in front of him. "Broderick, look at me. Look. At. Me," I said. He finally did. "We're having a baby. A little dragon baby. We're starting our family. I need you to be happy about this."

He closed his eyes, the tension in his shoulders softening. "I am. I swear, I am," he said. "I'm just terrified."

"Me too. I've never done this before, either. I've been around omega wolves giving birth for what feels like my whole life. but I'm still terrified. I think that's part of the adventure."

"It's a really shitty part," he said.

I laughed. "I know, but we're going to be great at this. Gale and Leonidas can do it. I think you can, too."

He rolled his shoulders back and scoffed. "I'll be a better father than them any day of the week."

I rolled my eyes, but if an alpha chest-thumping competition was what it took to snap him out of his funk, I'd take it.

Broderick's phone beeped, and he pulled it from his pocket.

"Everyone's in the library," he said. "Armant's back." The tension in his shoulders returned. "Good, we can tell them about that damn vampire."

This time, I let Broderick pick me up and carry me. I could talk later about how he would need to process his emotions into something more productive. For right now, I was still running on a high knowing that I was carrying my dragon's baby.

In the library, we found Armant sitting on the couch, the piece of paper I'd drawn the amulet on in his hand.

He stared at it, rotated it, stared at it some more, then rotated it back.

Broderick set me down and Armant stood and rushed over. "This is the amulet you saw?"

"Yeah," I said. "I didn't see it today, though. Did you, Broderick?"

"No. Bastard wore a turtleneck, like he's Steve-fucking-Jobs or something."

I almost laughed at the macho alpha behavior that Broderick displayed, but the situation didn't call for laughter. "Do you know what it is?" I asked.

"It's not supposed to exist." Armant said. "It's just a myth."

"Mythical creatures have myths and legends of their own?" Frost asked. He sat on the floor with Crispin, the little guy finally enjoying tummy-time, instead of screaming his little head off.

I sat down next to him, wanting to observe, knowing that in a few short months I'd have one of these creatures of my own to take care of. I had a lot to learn.

"What's it used for?" Broderick asked.

"It captures magic," Armant said.

"Interesting," Merek said.

"Barbaric," Armant countered. "If the wearer of the amulet kills a witch, their magic is then transferred to the amulet. That witch's power becomes theirs."

"That explains how he has his blinking ability, and how he was able to trick Gale into believing Frost had been kidnapped with some sort of illusion. What other powers are in there?" Merek asked.

"Old ones," Armant said. "In ancient times, magic was a lot stronger. My guess is he hasn't been able to harness the more powerful abilities inside of it. Or perhaps he doesn't know they are there.

And the two powers we know that he has, he may have acquired himself by killing a witch."

"That's terrifying," I said.

"No kidding. How can we destroy it? How can we destroy that vampire? He threatened my mate today." Broderick's fist clenched at his sides, like he was ready to fight right now.

"There is no way to destroy it," Armant said. "This amulet and its counterpart, the myth says that they were passed down from generation to generation, and that the guardians of them were never supposed to disclose their location."

"What does the other amulet do?"

"I don't know," Armant said. "It's supposed to be a counterpart to the other amulet."

"What do we know about the prophecy surrounding my mate?" Broderick asked.

I rolled my eyes at that. "Oh, please. It is not a prophecy. It's just a feeling that my mom had. And we've all pretty much decided it's just something she made up so that she could convince the wolf pack that it was perfectly okay to adopt a human."

Broderick's voice softened when he addressed me. "Then how did the vampire know about it?'

I shrugged. "Rumors. How does he know about anything?"

Broderick sat down beside me and grabbed my hand. "Mason. I don't feel like you're taking this very seriously right now."

At that moment, I seriously regretted ever talking to Broderick about how to effectively express his feelings using "I" statements.

"I am," I said, then I smiled. "I'm just too damn excited about having a baby."

"You're pregnant?" Frost asked.

I nodded.

"Oh, that's so exciting!" He launched himself at me and wrapped me in a hug.

"That has not been confirmed," Broderick said. "That's what the vampire said, but what the fuck does he know? How in the hell would he know that you're pregnant? You've never even gone into heat."

"What was the prophecy, exactly?" Leonidas asked me.

"It wasn't a prophecy," I said. "My mother saw me at some charity event that she was working. It was for foster kids in the area. She shook my hand and when she did, she had a vision that I would do something—she couldn't tell what—that would change the world as we know it. That's it."

"Who's 'we'?" Armant asked.

I shrugged. "I don't know."

"Well, is 'we' like humans? Is magic going to be exposed to the world or is 'we' paranormal creatures? Wolves, dragons, or some subset of that community?"

"Look, at the time when I was adopted, I was just so happy to have a family and a bed that I could sleep in for longer than a month or two. I didn't care about the vision my mother had seen at the time. I barely believed in all that supernatural stuff. Obviously, after living with a wolf pack, my skepticism had been effectively stamped down to nothing. We can ask her," I said.

"I did," Armant replied. "When I was visiting with the wolf pack. She said the same thing you did."

I rolled my eyes. "Well, then, why in the hell were you asking me about it?"

"I'd hoped that you might have some idea what it could mean."

"Well, I don't," I said. "I don't even believe it's true."

"Well, the vampire does and that's all that matters. If he has his sights set on Mason, we need to stop him," Gale interjected.

"No shit," Broderick said. "Armant, were you able to find out anything about him?"

"Not much. I spoke with two covens. Vampires don't generally live in large groups, but they do cluster together in families of three to five. Peter has never done that. He's always been a loner, and he also has a bad reputation for turning individuals without their consent."

"Oh, god. So, he's just been turning random people into vampires? And what, let's them wreak havoc?"

"No," Armant said. "He keeps them for a while, wherever he lives. And then no one knows what happens to them."

I sucked in a breath. "He kills them?"

"If they're lucky," Armant said.

My stomach turned at that. Broderick must have sensed my revulsion because he scooped me up into his arms. "You need to rest," he said.

"Oh, for god's sake. I'm just barely pregnant."

"We have no idea how far along you are. I don't recall you actually having a heat," he said.

I searched my memory for anything that could've remotely felt like what Flint and Frost had described to me when they were first mated to their dragons. "I can't think of anything either," I said.

Merek snorted. "Well, it's no wonder. The two of you haven't gone more than twenty minutes without fucking like rabbits for the past month. How would you ever notice if you were in heat?"

"So, we have no way of knowing how far along I am?"

We all looked to Armant.

"Why are you all looking at me?"

"Because you're the most knowledgeable," Frost said.

"Well, I don't know a damn thing about babies and heats. You and Flint or Valerie should know. Valerie will want to do a check up on him anyway."

I yawned and Broderick carried me out of the room. I would have protested, except a nap really did sound good right now.

"There is no prophecy," I told Broderick as we entered our suite.

He kissed my forehead. "We'll see. I want to ask your mom about it. And I'll call Valerie, so she can visit to give you an examination."

I grinned. "Mom's going to be pretty excited to be a grandma."

"I'm pretty excited to be a dad."

"Me, too."

•

Chapter Seven

Mason

A month later, I lay in bed with Broderick not wanting to get up. The pregnancy had been taxing on my body, not in the same way that Frost's had been. I wasn't extremely sick or fatigued but I seemed to be growing to extreme proportions. I looked about the same size at possibly two, maybe three, months pregnant that Frost had looked at almost five.

Broderick shook my shoulder. "Sweetheart, you have to get up."

"No. I'm too big to move."

He stroked my face with one hand, while the other rubbed over my abnormally large stomach. "You're gorgeous." He kissed my cheek, then my belly.

I wiggled away. "That tickles!" I said.

He chuckled. "Valerie's here. She wants to do an exam on you."

"Again?" I said.

"Yes, again." He picked me up, then set me on my feet.

I didn't even open my eyes. I stumbled toward the bathroom, feeling my way through the room. "Can I have a cup of coffee, please?"

"Since you asked so nicely, you can have one."

"Thanks. I'll meet you downstairs."

When I walked into the kitchen, Broderick and Valerie were there. Broderick had a huge plate of food for me, as well as a steaming cup of coffee.

"Damn," I said. "I wanted food, but this is a little overboard, Broderick."

"The article I read yesterday said that it's important for you to have protein and healthy fats. So, I made you an omelet with bacon, cheese, spinach, and mushrooms."

"It looks delicious, but how many eggs did you use?" I asked.

"Six."

Valerie threw her head back and laughed. "Well, no wonder your mate is so large if you're feeding him like this."

I agreed with her but took a bite just to appease my mate, knowing that he wouldn't let me rest until I had at least had a good portion of the meal he'd made for me. In the past month, Broderick had proven to be the epitome of an amazing mate. Always looking out for me, always making sure that I was happy. Not to mention the sheer amount of research he'd done on having a healthy pregnancy.

"Did you or Armant find out any more about how we can tell how far along I am?" I asked Valerie.

Valerie shook her head. "Dragon pregnancies last between four and five months. Both Frost and Flint made it to four and a half. Without knowing when you might have gone into heat, it's hard to tell."

"Well, how the hell do they tell with human babies?" Broderick asked.

"Usually by ultrasound or a last cycle date," Valerie said.

"Can we do an ultrasound?" Broderick asked.

"What are we going to do, order one off the internet and do it ourselves?"

Broderick shrugged. "I'll bet there's YouTube videos that could show us how."

Valerie nodded. "Sure. But being that dragon pregnancies are shorter than human pregnancies, even if we measured the child, there'd be no way of knowing when you were going to give birth or how far along you would be. Right now, you are between two and three months along. Based on your size, I'd lean more toward three."

Broderick growled. "I don't like not knowing."

Valerie rolled her eyes. "You're going to be raising a child, get used to being surprised by things."

"She has a good point," I said. "Any news on finding Peter or Molpe?"

"Molpe has gone completely underground," Armant said as he walked into the room. The usually stylishly dressed dragon wore tattered cargo pants and a white t-shirt stained with dirt and grime. "And we have a few leads on Peter. Apparently, he did not kill all the little creations he made, and some are still alive. But I haven't had any luck locating them. I'm on it, though."

"What happened to you?" I asked.

He looked down at himself as if he'd just now noticed his attire. "Well, the vampires I'm looking for don't exactly live in the upper echelons of society."

"I want to help track them down," Broderick said. "You shouldn't be out there by yourself."

"You need to stay here with your mate," Armant said to him. "We have this well in hand. Besides, I'm still chasing down leads on the amulet. If too many people start asking questions about it, we'll draw too much attention to it."

"Can't stand the thought of a one-of-a-kind piece of jewelry out there that's not in your possession?" Broderick chided.

Armant shrugged one shoulder. "Well, now that I know it actually exists, yes, I would prefer that someone who knows its purpose and its capabilities have it, so it doesn't fall into the wrong hands."

"So, it has nothing to do with the fact that it's a jewel that you don't have in your hoard?"

Armant rolled his eyes. "I will not apologize for my dragon's desire to fill our hoard with precious gems."

"Wait," I said. "You have a hoard of jewels? I assumed since you guys have never mentioned hoards, that it was just a myth."

"Generally, only jeweled dragons keep hoards," Broderick said. "The rest of us could care less about keeping things in our possession like gems and shiny objects. But, dangle something shiny in front of Armant's face, and he'll go to the ends of the earth to get it for himself."

Armant lifted his chin. "It's in my nature. I'm not going to apologize for that."

I laughed. "Can I see it? Like, where do you keep it? Or is that one of those things I shouldn't ask? Like, you would never reveal the location of your hoard?"

"I don't keep it all in one place," Armant said. "A lot of it is actually on display at museums or in some of my stores."

"Stores?" I realized just how little I knew about Armant. He'd always struck me as the studious type, spending his time in the library.

"Armant owns a chain of jewelry stores. That's his current business these days," Broderick explained.

"So, it doesn't bother you that your hoard is on display for all to see in a museum or whatever?"

"No," he said. "What's important is that it's mine, and I can see it whenever I want." Armant stared off into the distance. "And hold it, and touch it."

"Usually if we can't find Armant for a while, we'll find him in one of his vaults, rubbing diamonds all over his face."

"Like you're any better," Armant said. "Transforming into your beast of a dragon and laying on stone."

Broderick laughed. "Touché."

It was nice to see him and Armant having fun with each other, even if it was at each other's expense. For too long, my had mate acted too serious and refused to enjoy life. Now, it seemed that he was finally understanding that it was all about balance.

"Eat your breakfast," Broderick said and handed me a glass of milk. "It's important to get plenty of vitamins."

I took a sip of it, despite the fact that I was quite full. If it made him happy, then that's what I would do.

***

After I'd finished an adequate amount of my breakfast to satisfy Broderick, I made my way onto the deck where Flint and Frost were with Keegan and Crispin. The two of them watched Leonidas and Gale set up the tools and sawhorses they'd need to build the playset structure today.

Broderick had finally gotten around to getting the lumber delivered, and the three of them thought that they could complete it all in one day. I had my doubts, but it would be fun to watch. Either way, they refused to allow me to help though I could hold my own with a hammer and a saw. After all, on the wolf compound we built our own homes.

"Which one is going to lose his temper first, do you think?" Flint asked. He had his laptop open, trying to get some work done while also trying to keep Keegan from pressing all the buttons.

I gathered Keegan into my arms and tickled him. "Come over here and play with me, little guy."

Flint sighed. "Thank you."

"Normally, I'd put my money on Broderick. But for the past couple of weeks, he seems to have mellowed out. He rarely loses his temper anymore," Frost said.

I smiled. "He has his moments, this might be one of them. He gets all particular and picky when it comes to building stuff. Last week when he and Armant took out that wall between the library and the playroom, he had a few choice words to say about that 'damn jeweled dragon.'" I impersonated Broderick's booming voice. He must have heard me, because he looked up and shot me a grin. I waved.

"I'm going to bet Leo's going to start it on fire before the day's end," Flint said.

"He better not. We had a hell of a time getting that lumber here," I said.

"No kidding," Frost said. "I had to do all of the damn research on the delivery driver to make sure he wasn't some sort of covert vampire something or other."

"I can't wait for all of this business with Molpe and Peter to be behind us," I said.

"Me too," Frost said. "Gale refuses to talk about having more kids until they've been dealt with."

"Leo's the same way," Flint said.

"So, the crazy protectiveness doesn't end after the pregnancy?" I asked.

Both Flint and Frost shook their heads. "Nope. Just gets worse."

I rubbed a hand over my belly. "So many exciting things to look forward to."

Chapter Eight

Broderick

Something woke me from my deep slumber. I opened my eyes to complete darkness and listened for a sound, a movement that may have awoken me. Mason remained sound asleep in my arms, his back against my chest. My arm draped protectively over him and his protruding stomach.

I lifted my head from the pillow and listened. Nothing. The fan we usually kept going in the room had turned off, as well as the light we kept on in the adjoining bathroom, so Mason could wake up five times a night to pee without tripping over anything.

Something was wrong.

The power was out.

I carefully got out of the bed, trying not to wake my mate. Mason shifted in his sleep and hugged the pillow, still sleeping. I tip-toed out of the room. I needed to wake Merek if the power was out and the generators hadn't kicked in.

I walked down the hall to the stairwell. I flicked the light switch on the wall out of habit and the light turned on. I paused. The power wasn't out throughout the entire house. So, what was going on in my room?

My blood ran cold. *Mason.*

I ran, sliding on the wood floor, nearly missing the door to my room. I turned the knob, but the door wouldn't open. My dragon roared within me and I ripped the door from its hinges, tearing the door apart. Pieces of the frame splintering around me.

Mason was still in the room, but he wasn't alone.

"Shhhhh," Peter said.

Peter. Fucking vampire.

"Don't make a sound." He snapped his fingers and a glow illuminated the room just enough so I could see a dagger in his hand, right against Mason's throat. "Struggle, and he dies."

My heart thundered in my chest, but I didn't move a muscle, any flinch, any movement meant Mason's death, the death of our child.

Mason eyes opened wide as if he sensed my fear. When he met my gaze, the vampire grasped Mason's hand and pulled him to his feet.

"How did you get in here?" Mason asked.

"I've acquired a new skill, one that counteracted your witch's spell she had on the place. And luckily, a few little cuts to some wires was all I needed to break past your security system."

Mason opened his mouth as if to scream. Peter put a hand over his mouth. "If you wake the whole household and alert anyone else, I will kill you. If he makes a move" he gestured toward me, "I will kill you."

"You'll never make it out of here alive," Mason said through clenched teeth. He wrapped his arm protectively around his belly.

"That's true," Peter said. "But neither will you or your baby or your mate. We can do this the really simple way. You and I are going to leave, and your mate is going to stay here. Or if you want to put up a fight, I will kill your mate and I will still take you with me. Or I can kill both of you. Your choice. You have about ten seconds to make a decision."

Mason look to me. His eyes filled with unshed tears. "I— I," he said.

I swallowed the lump in my throat. I couldn't speak. I tried to launch for my mate or tackle the vampire to the ground and rid us of this mess once and for all. I didn't make it very far before the vampire took the dagger and plunged it into my stomach. He twisted it for good measure and pain ripped through my entire body.

Mason screamed, and then suddenly went silent.

My dragon roared within me, and I staggered to my feet. A hot stream of blood ran down my stomach. I let out a tremendous roar that should not have been possible in my human form. The sound shook the walls and parts of the ceiling cracked under the enormous pressure.

I couldn't think.

I couldn't breathe.

- I lunged for Peter again. He pushed Mason behind him. The dagger flew threw the air and lodged just below my collar bone before I could dodge out of the way. Then Peter and Mason disappeared into thin air.

I shifted, scales erupted on my skin as my dragon came to the surface. It's massive size too much for the house to contain. The walls caved in around me until they burst at the seams.

Then everything went black.

***

I heard Merek and Armant talking behind me, but their words couldn't penetrate the agony that ripped apart my soul.

Was this how Carrik had felt? No. It couldn't be. Mason had been kidnapped, but he was at least still alive. He had to be alive. I couldn't imagine any other scenario.

"Broderick! You need to wake up." Merek's voice filtered into my haze of consciousness.

I opened my eyes and blinked a few times, and the backyard came into focus. When did I get outside? How did I get outside?

I staggered to my feet, only to realize that I was in dragon form. I let out a whine, plopped back down on the ground, and then Merek and Armant looked at me. Merek came right up to where I lay.

"Snap out of it, Broderick, your mate needs you."

I unfurled my wings, ready to take off and find Mason. I'd go to the ends of the Earth if that was what it took to find him.

"No," Merek said. "You need to get back into your human form. Focus," he said.

I closed my eyes and transformed back.

"Finally," Armant said. "We've been trying to get through to you for several hours."

I put my head in my hands. "How long has it been?"

"Three hours since the power was cut."

"So that means three hours since Mason has been taken from me. What do we know?"

"Nothing," Armant said.

"Where are Gale and Leonidas?"

Armant looked away. "They took the kids and their mates to go check on Valerie."

"Are they okay?" I asked.

"Yes," Merek said. "We just had the kids leave as a precaution. I think you're going to have to do a bit of repair work on the house though. You took a sizeable chunk out of the south side."

That I could handle, as soon as I had my mate back. "Is Valerie okay? The vampire mentioned getting through her spell somehow. I wondered if that means…"

"He broke into her home and destroyed her totem. It's what she used to hold the protection spell in place. Thankfully, she wasn't there."

"I should have kept my mate safe, should have been prepared." I clenched my fists. "I will find that vampire and I will kill him."

"We," Armant said. "You're not doing this alone."

I opened my mouth to protest.

"No argument," Armant said. "We're a family. You'd do the same for my mate. You've done the same for Gale and for Leonidas's mate. You're going to accept help, whether you like it or not."

I nodded. "What can we do when Valerie gets here? I can try that scrying thing that Frost used to find Gale."

Merek nodded. "They should be back anytime."

I hated waiting. Hated knowing that my mate was out there with somebody else, and I couldn't protect them, him or our child.

"I have a lead on one of the vampires that Peter turned. He managed to escape. I've been trying to figure out a way to approach him without spooking him. But this situation might call for a little more force than I had anticipated," Armant said.

"Let's go then. Let's get him now," I said. I needed to do *something* to find my mate. I could not wait around.

Armant shook his head. "I need him alive and you're likely to tear him apart if he doesn't cooperate. I'll get him. I'll bring him back here."

"Do you think that's safe?" Merek asked.

"No, but I don't think we have a choice. And I don't want to waste any more time. If there is even the slightest chance this guy knows anything, it's worth a shot," Armant said.

"Please," I said. "Go. Be safe."

Faster than I could process in my mind, Armant changed into his dragon, shredding his clothing as he did so and took off into the air.

Now was not the time for stealth and subtlety.

"Is there anything else we can do?" I said.

"Come on inside. Eat something. You'll need your strength if you're going to take on a vampire. I'll grab my laptop. I haven't been able to find any information on Peter's holdings, but there's always a paper trail. If he owns property that he's taken his little creations to or Mason, we should be able to find it somehow."

I nodded, feeling extremely helpless in this situation. "I need to do something," I said.

Merek put a hand on my shoulder. "Trust your friends. Trust us to be able to help you. When the time comes, you'll be there to save your mate."

I nodded, unsure what else I could do.

***

It felt like days passed before Gale and Leonidas arrived back with Valerie. Luckily, she was fine, as were Frost, Flint and the kids. I apologized for scaring them, but they waved off my concerns.

"Can we try scrying for Mason?" I asked Valerie.

"We can," she said. "But I doubt it'll work. Peter's acquired some new skills and he's most likely blocked that magic by now."

I agreed with her, but nonetheless, we tried. For over an hour we poured over the map. I focused on Mason, my mate, my love, my life. I focused on how he made me feel, how I felt when he was happy.

Nothing.

The crystal never dropped to where he was located. After some time, I grew frustrated, but resisted the urge to throw the crystal across the room or tear up the map that laid out in front of me. Losing my temper would not do my mate any favors. I'd done enough damage to our room before Merek and Armant had thrown me outside.

"Every minute he's away," I said. "is another moment he's in danger."

Never mind the fact that the vampire obviously wanted Mason for himself. I assumed that he wouldn't harm Mason. But for how long? Was there a chance that he simply wanted to get rid of Mason, because he couldn't have him for himself? If he couldn't have him, then no one could.

I scrubbed my face with my hands. A roar sounded outside and we all leapt to our feet. Frost and Flint fled the room with the kids, going into a safer area, deeper in the house.

Merek and I rushed outside as Armant landed in the driveway. He had a nasty gash on his shoulder, that dripped blood over the driveway.

"What the fuck?" I said. "What happened to you?" I didn't even notice the person he held in his talons until Armant pushed him forward to Merek.

Merek grunted as the man ran into him. Chains wrapped around the man's wrists.

Armant changed back to his human form. The cut ran from his shoulder blade to the center of his chest. It looked deep and painful. Valerie rushed at him with a towel of some sort. "Good Goddess. What happened?"

"That's one of Peter's little creations. The one that escaped," Armant said.

"Fuck you, dragon. I'll never go back to him. I got free once, I'll get free again." He struggled against Merek's hold. The guy was slimmer in build and short, but extremely feisty. His skin was pale, and his dark brown hair appeared greasy, like he hadn't been able to wash it in a while. His clothes were dingy and rundown.

"Where in the hell did you find him?" Merek asked.

"You don't want to know," Armant said. "Little fucker put up quite a fight. Who in the hell knows how to wield a sword anymore these days anyway?"

"It's a good skill to have," the man said. "You should try it sometime." Sarcasm dripped from his words like a weapon.

"Let's take him inside," I said. I wanted to shake him to find out what he knew. But I also didn't want to get my hopes up that he would have any sort of information. The man appeared homeless, and he obviously hadn't showered in a while. Any physical damage I could do to him during interrogation would be cruel and unnecessary. He'd already been broken but was still standing.

Inside the house, we set the man down at a table in the library. He placed his chained hands on the table and refused to speak.

"Tell us about Peter," Merek demanded.

He shook his head. "I won't go back. I'll die first. I've tried everything, but surely there's a way that a vampire can commit suicide. I'll find it. I will."

My eyebrows raised at that. "We need to find Peter. We don't want to send you back there. We just want your help."

"Fuck that," the man said. "I don't trust any of you freaks. Pick up a guy at a bar one time and end up chained in his dungeon for six months. That's what trusting people gets you. I won't do it. Not going to say a word." He shook his head, frantically. His greasy hair flopped in front of his face.

Valerie reached across the table and tried to put her hand on his. He flinched away. "Don't touch me, witch! I know that's what you are. I can tell these things, now. Witches. Dragons. Weird ass Sirens that make god-awful screeching noises when you make them angry. All of you, freaks."

"What can you tell us about Peter?" Armant asked. His shoulder almost completely healed now. He'd pulled on a pair of sweatpants and cleaned most of the blood off his chest.

"Nothing. Not telling you anything. Just like I wasn't going to tell you when you picked me up at my home. Not saying a word."

Armant scoffed. "You call that a home? You were living in the sewer system under the city."

"I can't be out in the sun very long, idiot. Don't you know that?"

"There are herbs you can take," Valerie said carefully. "So, you can endure the sunlight longer."

He looked at her like she'd grown two heads. "How in the fuck am I supposed to know that? Do you think I wanted to be a blood-sucking freak? Do you think I wanted to drink blood in order to live? Well, I don't. But that's what happened."

"Look." I leaned toward him. Everybody took a sharp intake of breath, like I was going to lunge across the table and tear the guy apart. No, I wasn't about to do that. This vampire, this man, that had been turned against his will, he knew things about Peter that we didn't. He knew secrets, and he just might be able to help take Peter down. "Listen, Peter has taken my mate." No response. "I don't know what he did to you or why, but I can tell you want revenge. And I can promise you that if you help me find him, it'll be the last time Peter hurts anybody. I will kill him."

The man continued to shake his head. "Nope. Not gonna say anything. Don't trust any of you."

"What's your name?" I asked.

He stared at me for a moment. Stunned into a silence.

"Jay," he said quietly.

I wasn't sure if it was his real name or just what he was going to go with for right now, but I'd take it. "Jay," I said. "I know this is all probably a shock to you. I'm sure before Peter got a hold of you, you were a normal guy with hopes and dreams and plans for the future. Peter fucked that all up. And for that, I'm sorry. But my mate, Mason, he's human, too. He has hopes and dreams, a future. He's carrying our child."

"What the fuck?" Jay said.

I may have said too much. Obviously he didn't know about male pregnancies.

"That's not important right now. What's important is that you help me find him. Please." I begged.

He shook his head. "Nope, not happening."

I pulled out my phone and found the most recent picture of Mason I had taken. It was a selfie of him and I on the rocks in our clearing. Just laying there smiling. "Please," I said. "That's Mason. That's my mate. I can't live without him. If you help me, if you help us find him, I swear I will help you with whatever you need. If you need money, I will give it to you. If you need a home, we'll find you one. If you need help, we'll be there. No matter what. No questions asked. Just please, help me find Mason."

Jay swallowed thickly. "Fine," he said. "I want to know if there's a way to reverse this. I don't want to be *this* anymore."

I looked over at Valerie and then to Merek and Armant. That was one thing I couldn't give. "I'm sorry. There isn't a way to reverse it," I said. "But we can help you cope. Being a vampire doesn't mean you have to be a monster like Peter. There are plenty of good vampires in the world. We can help you find ways to get access to the blood you need to live without harming anyone."

"I haven't killed anyone," Jay said quietly. "I've been living off rats in the sewer. But I'm starving." He groaned. "Just being around people makes me hungry." His fangs dropped as if on cue.

"We can help you with that," I said.

Valerie disappeared, blinking out of the room. Hopefully in search of something that would satisfy Jay's need.

"I need my laptop," he said. "Well, it's not even my laptop. It's Peter's. I stole it when I left. The idiot thought I was just a stupid street kid that he could kidnap and do whatever he wanted with. But I didn't survive on the streets my whole life just to be some pet to a vampire in his stupid mansion. If I get his laptop, we can look through the files on there. There's a lot of information about the properties he owns. Including the one he kept me at. We might be able to find where he's keeping this mate of yours."

I closed my eyes and hope filled me. "Thank you," I said.

"Don't thank me yet. We haven't saved your mate. And I'll expect you to hold up your end of the bargain."

"We will," I said.

***

"We've got three properties that he could possibly be at," Merek said hours later after we'd retrieved the laptop. It had now been nearly eight hours since Mason had been taken and I could barely take it any longer. "One is where he kept Jay. I personally think we can rule that one out. He's probably abandoned it by now. So, it's between the other two."

I stared at the addresses. Both were equidistant from here.

"Why don't we split up? Armant and Leonidas can go to one. You and I will go to the other," Merek said.

"What are we going to do when we get there?" I asked.

"Save your mate. Torch the place. Kill that vampire once and for all."

Sounded like a solid plan to me. "What about Molpe?" I asked. "Do you think she's helping Peter right now?"

"Hard to tell. I'm beginning to think he might just be obsessed with your mate, and that's what's driving all of this," Armant said.

I nodded. "I got that same vibe." Just the thought of Peter putting his hands on my mate had scales breaking out on my skin. I took a deep breath, pushing my dragon back. "Alright. Let's go." I ripped the paper in two and handed the address to Armant. "Call us if you think he's there. We'll have our phones on us. Don't engage until we get there."

Armant nodded. He shook my hand, then wrapped his arm around on my shoulder in a half hug. "We're going to get him back, I promise."

"Thank you," I said. "All of you." I looked around at Leonidas, Gale, Armant, and Merek, each of my friends nodded their heads in solidarity.

"Of course. You would do the same for us," Merek said.

"You have done the same for us," Gale said.

"Let's head out. We don't have any time to waste."

I stripped off all my clothes before I even got outside. I was barely clear of the door, when I started transforming, then took off into the air, beating my wings wildly in the direction I needed to go to get to my mate. To get to Mason.

I would not fail.

Chapter Nine

Mason

I paced around the room that Peter had left me in. I'd tried every door, every window. All locked. The entire room was black, the trim, the walls, the furniture. I was surprised there wasn't a coffin in the corner to sleep in. Instead, there was a regular four poster king-size bed. The thought of lying in it made my skin crawl. Peter had been in there, and I didn't want to touch anything that he'd touched.

The only light in the room came from an old-style candelabra in the corner of the room. I rolled my eyes at that. I knew Peter was a vampire, but damn, he seemed to be taking the image a bit too far with his surroundings. Would it kill him to put a little lighting in here?

I'd stumbled more than a few times, running into end tables, a couch, and god knows what else.

"Let me out of here!" I screamed.

It wasn't the first time I had shouted since Peter had left me in there. And I got the same result as every other time. Silence.

I didn't even know how big this place was or where it was located, since we'd popped right into this room and then he'd popped out again. I didn't even know if he was still in the same building as me.

I sat down on the couch and rubbed a hand over my belly. "It's going to be fine, little one. I promise." I felt movement underneath my skin and my hand went still. Oh, god. Not now.

Movement meant that I'd be having the baby soon, according to Flint and Frost. But that couldn't happen, not yet. I needed to get out of here first. I knew Broderick would come for me. I had no idea how they'd find me, but I knew they would. That didn't stop me from continuing to try every exit to free myself, though.

Peter popped back in and startled me. "What the fuck!" I said.

"Sorry. I didn't mean to scare you. I got the tools I needed, so when it's time, I'll be ready." A look of pure evil came over his face.

Oh, fuck. My blood ran cold. "Time for what?" I said. "Let me go. Broderick will find you and he will kill you. Just let me go. Leave us alone. Live your own damn life."

Peter shook his head. "I'm sorry, Mason. I can't do that. I've come too far."

"What do you want from me?" I asked.

Peter took a step toward me and I backed away until I was cornered against the wall. His eyes widened, and fury set in on his face. I'd never seen such a complete switch of emotion.

"You all think you're so great. Dragons getting gifted with their mates after what they did to the world years ago? It's a fucking joke. Since five dragons were on good behavior for the past two thousand years, suddenly they get to find their mates. You don't know how good you have it. Finding your mate, living happily ever after. While the rest of us suffer, searching to the ends of the earth for our own mates, only to come up empty handed. Every time I think I've found the one, he ends up belonging to someone else. It's bullshit. I'm tired of it. We'll see how you feel after your mate is dead. Then you can be mine. We may not have the mate bond Mason, but we could still be together."

"I will never be with you." I put a hand over my stomach.

He eyed my belly, making me want to shrink away from him even more.

"I've always considered myself something of a scientist, you know," he said. "I wonder what would happen to your baby, if I changed you right now. Took a bite out of your neck, sucked your blood until you ran dry, and turned you into a creature like me. Do you think we could possibly have the first dragon-vampire hybrid?"

"You're insane," I said. I looked away from him. I didn't want to hear any more of what he had to say.

"We'll see," he said. He opened his bag that he'd carried in and laid out a few objects. I couldn't help but look at them and wished I hadn't. One was a scalpel. The other a bone saw.

"What in the fuck?" I scrambled away from him.

"This isn't going to hurt. As long as your dragon is still alive, then you two are bonded. You'll have his healing ability. He might not be the one to cut that baby out of you, but the results will be the same. It will be painless, and you'll heal completely." He paused for a moment. "I think. We'll find out together."

"You are mad," I said.

He shrugged. "I suppose. When you live as long as I have, things get a little crazy."

I did the only thing I could think of and I upended the table he'd laid the tools on and ran for the door. I tried the knob, shaking it furiously. Nothing happened. I couldn't get out. I pounded my fists on it again and again, screaming for help.

Peter threw his head back, laughing behind me.

***

I had no idea how much time had passed. I'd stopped beating on the door a while ago and settled on the couch after Peter had disappeared from the room. I forced myself to sleep, to conserve my energy, and to hopefully keep my baby from making an early appearance.

Peter popped in and out of the room, but I didn't bother speaking with him, or even looking at him. He'd taken the tools with him, so I couldn't even use them to defend myself. I'd looked around the room, trying to find something that I could use, but there was nothing. I'd even tried tearing a leg off the end table to use as a club, but it wouldn't budge.

When I heard the roar outside for the first time, I knew my mate was coming, and then the house began to shake with each mighty roar of my stone dragon. The chandelier that hung from the ceiling in the center of the room danced.

I sprang to my feet, ready to leave with Broderick the minute I saw him.

Instead, Peter appeared, dagger in hand. He grabbed me by the wrist and pulled me out of the room.

"I think your mate and his dragon friends might be a little smarter than I gave them credit for. No matter," he said. "I'll just kill him now and be done with it. Then you'll be free of that bond, and you and our child will live happily ever after, with me.

I staggered and tripped as Peter held the dagger to my neck and pushed me forward. I felt a prick of pain and warm liquid trickling down the side of my neck.

Broderick and Merek were just touching down when Peter and I made it outside. Peter screamed at them. "Come any closer, and I will kill him."

I held myself as still as I could, trying to prevent any more harm to myself and my child. I didn't want to give Peter any reason for the blade to slip.

Broderick transformed first. "Give him back, Peter."

"No," he said. "You don't deserve him. He's too good for you."

"You're not wrong," Broderick said. "But he is my mate, not yours. Why don't you let him decide where he wants to go?"

Peter laughed at that. "He doesn't even know just how special he is or how special the baby he carries is. Neither of you know. He's going to change the world and I'm going to be at his side when he does it. Not you."

My gaze met Broderick's and I shook my head ever so slightly. I didn't want him to do anything stupid that might get himself hurt. I had no idea what to do in this situation besides plead with him with my eyes to not get hurt. I couldn't bear it if something happened to him.

"Why don't you let him go and we'll fight for him," Broderick said. "Hand to hand combat. No tricks, no weapons, no help. I won't even transform into my dragon. Drop the dagger and let's do this."

"Fine," Peter said. "If that's the way you want to play it. Let's go." He pushed me away from him, pulling the dagger away from my neck. I landed on the ground, cradling my stomach to protect it from the fall.

I stood just in time to see Peter launching himself at Broderick. His superhuman strength evident in the twenty-foot leap. Peter bared his fangs and slashed at Broderick with his hands. He delivered blow after blow to Broderick's face and torso.

I picked up the dagger that Peter had dropped, ready to jump in and help my mate. Merek held me back.

"No," he said. "They agreed to a fair fight, we can't interfere."

I watched helplessly as they fought.

Broderick landed a solid punch to Peter's midsection and the vampire stumbled back. His eyes widened, and he retaliated, lunging himself at Broderick in full force. They seemed evenly matched, despite Broderick's immense strength. Peter had the speed. He landed a few hard blows to Broderick's face, but they healed quickly, barely even trickling blood before the cuts closed. Broderick landed a solid sucker punch to Peter's face, and he stumbled back. Broderick didn't let up, kicking Peter until Peter laid on the ground, barely able to stand.

Peter's face was badly bruised. His shirt and pants were marred with tears and streaks of blood.

"Stay down," Broderick said. "You lose." He turned toward me.

Peter jumped to his feet. He had something in his hand, a rectangular type device that I didn't recognize right away until it hit Broderick solidly in the back and he convulsed.

A taser.

I ran to Broderick's side as he fell limply to the ground. I pushed Peter, causing him to stumble back. I'd taken him more by surprise than actual strength.

Broderick shook violently on the ground. His eyes rolled in the back of his head. I held his face in my hands. "Broderick? Can you hear me?"

Merek stood by, preventing Peter from getting near us.

"Step away, dragon," Peter said. "This fight was to the death and I would like to finish it."

"No," Merek said. "You cheated."

"Fine," Peter said. "I'll kill you first and then the stone dragon."

Peter lunged forward with his taser, catching Merek solidly in the chest, like he had done with Broderick, but he didn't count on it backfiring. Instead of sending an electric jolt through Merek it reversed and jolted Peter instead. He flew into the air landing nearly twenty feet away from Merek.

"What the fuck," I said.

Merek shrugged. "I think I have a gift for electricity."

Broderick groaned, finally opening his eyes. He pushed himself up and I helped him get to his feet. Peter was just about to stand again when Broderick reached him. He grabbed him by the throat and held him in the air. Peter's hands clutched at the one Broderick gripped around his neck. His feet kicked wildly as he tried to get out of Broderick's hold.

He opened his mouth to speak and uttered one word, "Molpe."

I picked up the dagger Peter had held to my neck, threatening my life. I handed it to Broderick. I turned away as Broderick plunged it into Peter's chest, but I heard the finality in the thump as

Peter's body hit the ground.

Then Broderick's arms were around me. "He's not going to bother us anymore," Broderick said.

"Thank you," I said. "I knew you'd come."

"Always," he said. He pulled me tight against him. "I will always come for you."

A scream pierced the air and we looked to where Peter's lifeless body lay.

"You killed him!" Molpe screeched.

Broderick pushed me behind him and Merek stepped to his side.

"You'll be next Molpe."

She narrowed her eyes as if carefully weighing the odds of her success if she were to pick a fight right now. "Not today, dragons. This isn't over. I told Peter that damn human he was obsessed with would get him killed. But he didn't listen. Now look at him." She bent down, reached inside his shirt and pulled out the amulet. "As long as I have this, that's all that matters."

Merek lunged for her, but she disappeared before he could grab her.

"Damn it," he said.

At that moment, the baby decided to kick again or whatever the hell it was doing that caused me to feel its movements.

Broderick stepped back. He stared from my stomach, back to my face again. "Was that…?"

I nodded.

"Holy shit. How long has that been happening?"

I shrugged. "Since I got here."

"Do you think you're in labor? How soon?"

"I have no idea. Could be right now, could be a few hours from now?"

"Are you in any pain?"

I shook my head. "No, but I wouldn't mind getting home so we could at least be there when Junior decides to make his appearance."

Broderick nodded. He looked over to Merek.

"I'll take care of this," he said, already lighting Peter's body on fire.

Broderick transformed, and I carefully climbed onto his back. He took off, taking me home.

Thankfully, the flight was quick. Broderick wasted no time, flying as fast as he could back to Dragon Headquarters. As soon as we touched down and I slid off his back, the pain ramped up. I clutched my stomach and fell to the ground.

Broderick was at my side, instantly in his human form. I pushed at him. "Change back! Change back! It's time!"

He held my shoulders. "Are you sure?"

I glared at him. "Yes, I'm fucking sure!"

Frost and Flint rushed outside. "It's time," they both said. They shouted at Broderick, "Change!"

He did.

I lay flat on my back in the middle of the driveway. Pain and pressure erupted in my stomach and lower back. The steady throb of pressure was almost unbearable. I searched for my dragon and found him staring at me. "Do it," I said. "Let's meet our baby."

A low rumble worked through his chest and he lifted a claw.

I didn't feel anything after that. The pain melted away and the next thing I knew I heard a baby cry. Broderick, still in his dragon form, held our child in his hand. He stood there, just staring at the bundle in his claw. He changed back, and I could see our child in his arms.

I reached my arms up. "Let me see."

Our child let out a wail, and Broderick continued to stare in complete wonder.

"It's a girl," he whispered.

"What?" Merek's voice startled me. I hadn't even realized he'd landed and transformed.

I looked around to see that everyone was here. Armant, Leonidas, Gale, Merek, Flint and Frost, even Valerie was there standing next to Broderick, holding a blanket, ready to wrap our child. Her eyes wide with shock.

"Well, that should change the world as we know it," Armant said.

That's when I realized the vision my mother had, the prophecy that Peter talked about it, was this. Our child.

"The first female dragon," I said, and Broderick looked at me.

"Yes," he said. He knelt at my side.

I sat up and took our child from him. "Our baby girl." I grinned at him and he grinned back.

"I didn't think of any girl names," he said.

"Harley," I said. "It means rock meadow."

He smiled, and a tear slipped out of the corner of his eye. "Harley Cara. First girl dragon."

***

Hours later, we all gathered in the library.

I held Harley in my arms. We'd cleaned her up and wrapped her in a blanket.

"I guess we might have to buy some clothes for her," I said to Broderick. "We can't utilize many of the hand-me downs we got from Flint and Frost."

He chuckled. "Yeah. This is kind of a game changer." He put his arm around me and stared at our daughter. "Why don't you let me take her and you can get some rest? I'm sure you're exhausted."

"I am," I said. "But I want to just keep watching her. She's so beautiful."

Broderick kissed my forehead. "Yes, she is. You're amazing."

I grinned. "Thanks. You know, I never really believed when my mom said that I'd do something that would change the world as we know it, but she just might have been right."

"I'd say so," Armant said. "There's never been a girl dragon. It'll be interesting to see what that will be like."

"What are we going to do about Molpe?" Broderick asked.

"Who knows?" Armant said. "Right now, I'm focused on either destroying the amulet or finding a way to hide it where no one can use it."

"What about Jay?" I asked.

Broderick had told me about the vampire that he and Armant had questioned to find out more about Peter and where he was keeping me. I felt for the man. His whole life had been turned upside down and he'd been used as a pawn for whatever game Peter was playing.

"We'll see what he wants to do. He's expressed some interest in going to the wolf pack and living amongst them for a while. He might have some luck there living a more 'normal' life. At least he wouldn't be alone."

I nodded. "He wouldn't be the only vampire. We have a couple of betas who are mated to vampires. Have you spoken with Jericho?"

"Yes," Broderick said. "I called him after you were taken, and Gale called him when we got back. He'd be here now, but Cody woke from his coma two days ago."

"Really? How is he? Has he said anything about Molpe? What does he know?"

Harley let out a squeak and I turned my attention back to her.

"Take it easy, Mason. We can speak with Jericho soon. We'll have to touch base anyway after all that happened today."

"I'll be heading that direction soon anyway," Armant continued. "One of my stores just hired a new appraiser and I think he might be able to help me to locate the other amulet. If it exists out there, this guy will be able to find it."

"One thing's for sure," Broderick said as he tightened his hold on me and Harley. "We have to find it before Molpe does."

Everyone nodded at that.

I relaxed into Broderick's embrace. The issues with Molpe could be dealt with at a later date, right now I reveled in my mate's embrace. Excited and scared for what the future might hold for us, as the parents of the only female dragon to ever exist.

"Rest, mate. I've got you and Harley. I'm never letting you go."

I closed my eyes. Broderick had me.

Mpreg Titles by Jena Wade

Rochadale Security

The Bodyguard's Charge (https://www.amazon.com/dp/B07R6BXXJD)
The Bodyguard's Relationship (https://www.amazon.com/dp/B07STJYFJS)
The Bodyguard's Professor (with Lorelei M. Hart) (https://www.amazon.com/Bodyguards-Professor-Romance-Rochdale-Security-ebook/dp/B07TTP3BCB)
The Bodyguard's Assistant
The Bodyguard's Technician

Millerstown Moments

Dashboard Lights (https://www.amazon.com/gp/product/B07MHFQQ3F)
All Revved Up (https://www.amazon.com/dp/B07N16DR5G)
Crying Out Loud (with Lorelei M. Hart) (https://www.amazon.com/gp/product/B07NKXJPRM)
Anything For Love (https://www.amazon.com/Anything-Love-Romance-Millerstown-Moments-ebook/dp/B07PKLFSKR)
Life is a Lemon (with Lorelei M. Hart) (https://www.amazon.com/Life-Lemon-Romance-Millerstown-Moments-ebook/dp/B07PYG9VT7)

Box Set with Heaven Can Wait short story (https://www.amazon.com/Millerstown-Moments-Complete-Boxset-Romance-ebook/dp/B07VGKWVJZ/)

Vale Valley

Picture Purrfect (https://www.amazon.com/dp/B07MM2TP6T)
The Cat & The Hound (https://www.amazon.com/dp/B07T6KW82Y)

Dragons Series

Dragon's Fire (http://www.amazon.com/dp/B07GGVSV11)
Dragon's Ice (https://www.amazon.com/dp/B07H73CT81)
Dragon's Stone (https://www.amazon.com/dp/B07HQCVV6S)
Dragon's Jewel (https://www.amazon.com/dp/B07K4YBQ7R)
Dragon's Spark (https://www.amazon.com/dp/B07KW2XNLG)

Directions Series

Up to Code (https://www.amazon.com/dp/B07DBL3W83)
Down to Earth (https://www.amazon.com/dp/B07DZB2PXK)
Back to You (https://www.amazon.com/dp/B07FXNV5MS)

Boxset (https://www.amazon.com/Directions-Book-Boxset-Sweet-Romance-ebook/dp/B07VCG2RXH)

Shorts

Alpha Student (https://www.amazon.com/dp/B07D7GGXZF)
Alpha Doctor (https://mailchi.mp/9b658a089de7/signup)

Jena Wade

Jena lives in Michigan with her husband, two dogs, and three children. By day she works as a web developer and at night she writes. She was born and raised on a farm and spends most of her free time outdoors, playing in the garden or tending to her landscaping.

Find out more about the author at http://www.thejenawade.com/.

Follow Jena on Facebook (https://www.facebook.com/jena.wade.7528) or Twitter (https://twitter.com/thejenawade).

Subscribe to Jena's Newsletter (https://mailchi.mp/9b658a089de7/signup)(she promises not to spam).

CPSIA information can be obtained
at www.ICGtesting.com
Printed in the USA
LVHW102032130522
718732LV00016B/1475